THE GIVEN DAY

THE GIVEN DAY

Robert van Gulik

1986

The Given Day was first published
(in English) privately by Robert van Gulik
(Kuala Lumpur, Malaysia; 1964)

The first American edition
was published as a limited hardcover
printing of 300 copies
in 1984 by Dennis McMillan

Postscript copyright © 1983 by
Janwillem Van de Wetering

Cover design by William L. McMillan

First paperback edition published December 1986

Dennis McMillan Publications
1995 Calais Dr. No. 3
Miami Beach, FL 33141

THE WRONG ADDRESS

"Here the bridges are different, Lina. Over there we had bridges too, and even canals, down town. But here in Amsterdam, a bridge over a canal, that's different. They change, you see, the canals and the bridges. They change with the time of the day, and with the time of the year."

"And with your mood, I suppose," she says, evenly. She pushes a lock of her raven-black hair under her close-fitting red hat that is wet with the drizzle. For the winter goes on. We had a white January, and February is wet : wet and cold. Leaning her elbows on the iron railing of the bridge, she looks down the old canal, lined by bare winter trees and bare iron lamp-posts; and by the gabled fronts of the high, narrow houses, shrouded by the gathering dusk. The few people that are about hurry along, keeping close to the houses, their heads bent.

Suddenly she turns her large black eyes on me and says, pensively :

"Strange that it's only six weeks since we came here. It seems so much longer. This drizzle could have been falling for months on end. I can't imagine that on Java, in the monsoon, when we were sitting on our front verandah, we couldn't see the garden for the solid sheet of rain. Do you remember that we . . . " Her voice trails off.

I do remember. Although it's longer ago now than six weeks — many years, in fact. I remember the days of the rain, and the days of the burning sun. I remember the first days, and I remember the last — particularly the first and the

1

last. Also the many days and nights of the years and months that were in between. I remember, because I carefully reconstructed them, the days and the nights, leisurely choosing them from the past, one by one. That is why I can exchange remembrances without missing a single clue, standing on the bridge over the canal and talking with the woman by my side who is dead.

Now she sighs and she says, wistfully:

"I love these old, solemn houses with their stepgables and their high doorsteps with those quaint iron railings. Look, some houses seem to lean forward, bend towards the canal, almost tenderly. Why should we go back?"

I know what I said in reply.

"You never belonged here, Linette", I said, "and I don't belong here either. Not any more. My parents have died, my relatives and my old friends have died or left. There's only the two of us. And we shall be happy, dear, over there."

Did you shiver, then? I don't know. But I do remember that you pressed your shoulder close against mine, on the bridge over the canal; a lonely pair in the February drizzle, at dusk.

"Let's not go back there," you said. "Let's stay here in Amsterdam, in your own town. You know so much about the law and all that, so you could make a living here too, couldn't you? Why go back to Java which I have come to loathe and where Effie ... where Effie died?"

"And why should you want to stay in Amsterdam, where I courted Effie, and where I made love with her?"

Why does one say such things to the woman one loves? Why did I say words that hurt, first to Effie, in the early years, and to Lina, in the later years? Say them to the women I loved and who are dead? I try to draw on my cigarette, but it has become wet. I throw the butt into the dark water of the canal, then I pull the sagging rim of my black felt hat deeper down, and I put the collar of my mackintosh up. It's not yet dark, my night-life shouldn't have begun. Lina shouldn't be there, not yet; neither should Effie. But perhaps Effie is coming early today, because it is February the 28th, the last day of a cold and wet, dreary February. For it was on that date that, so many years ago, I told Effie that I loved her. When I was seeing her home, I paused under the lamp-post, and I told her. She looked quickly to the left and right, and then she kissed me, and our cheeks were cold and wet from the rain, and her lips were warm and wet. Yes, it was about six o'clock, and there were no people about, otherwise she wouldn't have kissed me, under the lamp-post. The clock on the curb says it's five to six now. Only one hour to get through : one hour in which I must restore the balance between the day-life and the night-life. For at seven I shall be at the club and dining with my three friends; and then I am safe. We shall dine together at the cosy corner table, near the chimney. Only one hour to get through. A drink will help, perhaps.

I walk down the curved bridge, muttering a curse as I nearly lose my footing on the slippery cobblestones. Peering through the drizzle I see a reddish glow over a door farther down the street : the sign of a bar.

It's an old-fashioned pub, very small, very warm. It smells as it should smell, of raw Schiedam gin, damp clothes, tobacco and sawdust. About eight men stand at the high counter of neatly scoured wood, packed close together. There are no chairs, for one doesn't come here to sit. One comes to drink, because one needs it, as I am needing it now. For my eyes are blurred and my heart is thumping against my ribs, as

3

always on the bad days: on the days when I fear I shall lose control over the past, and when my thoughts go in frantic zigzags, or in sloppy, hopeless circles. I find room between an elbow in navy-blue, and an elbow in rough, well-worn tweed.

The publican's massive, hairy hand pushes a stemglass over to me. As he refills the glass by the navy-blue elbow, he asks in a rumbling voice:

"Why should today be different? To me, today is the same as every day."

"Because tomorrow means money," the navy-blue says in a high, reedy voice. "One day extra-money. For me."

The publican grunts. "Old or young?" he asks me.

"Old Schiedam."

"For me, it just means a day extra-work," the tweed elbow grumbles, "seeing that I am paid by the month. Another of the same, Jan!"

"You shouldn't complain," the publican tells him sourly. "Working for the city, that means a steady income. And a fat pension, when you retire."

"When you retire, Jan," the navy-blue says in his high-pitched voice, "you'll buy yourself a real house, on Richmen's Row!" He bursts out in a cackling laughter.

The warmth of the strong liquor spreads slowly through my cold limbs. I am beginning to feel better already, and I dare to widen my range of vision. When I have raised my head I see that the publican is a giant of a man, wedged in between the counter and the high cupboard with shining bottles behind his broad back. He has a florid round face with a drooping moustache. As he mechanically refills my empty glass he gives the navy-blue a nasty look.

4

Someone further down the row tells a joke. I don't get the point but I join the general laughter and down my third glass. Why should I worry? Doesn't everybody lead a double life? On the one hand the actual, daily routine. On the other, the life we imagine we ought to be living, or the life we might yet be living — if we only could summon that extra-bit of courage. And those second lives are important, for it is those we turn to for support in doubt and anxiety. Moreover, I am fully entitled to my second life. I am entitled to rebuild the past, because that's the only way I might prove that I am not a murderer. How could I be a murderer? I, who abhor, who loathe, violence and cruelty? Effie died, and small Bubu died, and Lina died, but I only committed mistakes. And I try to make up for those mistakes. At night.

During daytime I am a sedate ex-colonial official who leads a sedate, well-ordered life. During daytime I am a book-keeper in the Byenkorf, the department store. In my small, glass-walled office I write neat figures in neatly ruled ledgers: a restful, soothing work. For these figures have a purpose, a clearly-defined, fixed purpose. At half-past five I go home to my indifferent bed-sitting-room and I look at the evening paper till my old landlady serves up my indifferent meal, on my writing desk. When she has gone, and when I take up my fork and knife, the other life begins. Sometimes Effie sits opposite me, sometimes Lina. Not small Bubu, of course, for she eats first, with our Javanese nurse. I say all the words I should have said but never said, and I listen carefully to all the words they said and which I should have listened to. Now I have time, all the time in the world. Sometimes Effie and Lina don't come, and then I listen to a good concert on the radio, or I read: serious, soothing books, on philosophy or on religion. Especially on Buddhism, for Buddhism teaches that life is suffering. Never on history, for historical works give me a hollow feeling, deep in the pit of my stomach. They remind me that there is no purpose and that there never was one. The other books are soothing and they help to pass the time when my visitors don't come and I am alone. I can read those books in an impersonal manner because their terms don't apply. Perhaps their address is wrong, or maybe my address is wrong. It could be either way. I keep an open mind in these matters.

On the fifteenth and on the last day of every month I go to the club to have dinner there with my three friends, the doctor, the lawyer and the journalist. The doctor is a Catholic, the lawyer a Protestant. The journalist is something in between, and I am nothing. A common desire for non-committal talks on non-committal subjects brought us together. We know next to nothing about each other's private lives.

A loud burst of laughter startles me from my thoughts. The publican has placed his fat finger on the smudged leaf of the wall-calendar, under today's date, the 28th. He says in an aggrieved voice:

"And then I told the ornery bastard, look here, you, I says, you can see the date for yourself, can't you?" He takes his finger away. "But that ..."

I don't hear the rest. For by removing his finger he has uncovered a large figure. The figure 29. It grows larger and larger before my horrified eyes. Suddenly I break out in a cold sweat. This year is a leap-year, and consequently February has twenty-nine days. Tonight of all nights I shan't dine at the club. I shall be alone. Alone with the past that is getting out of control.

Abject fear makes my stomach heave. I can't be sick here in this pub, I must go outside, hurry. I manage to ask the

6

publican what I owe him, and I pay. The last thing I see as I am fleeing is that the gap between the navy-blue and the tweed elbow has closed. I am shut out.

The cold wind bites into my hot face. It has stopped raining, and there are many people about now, all in a hurry, their heads bent. I also bend my head and hurry along. And I pull the rim of my hat very low. Ordinarily no one will give me a second look: a tall thin man with graying temples, gray eyes, small gray moustache — all gray, a neutral gray. But on my bad days I have to be careful, for then I will think aloud, and my face becomes disfigured by a long red scar, right across my forehead where a Jap prison guard hit me with his rifle-butt, just a little too hard. The other scars don't matter. They are on my back, my arms and my legs, and they don't show.

From time to time I look up, hoping to see a quiet side-street. But I see only broad streets ahead, crammed with traffic and people and garish lights. I know from long experience that there's only one way to slow down my thoughts, which whirl around at ever increasing speed. That is a sober appraisal of simple facts. It is done somewhat like this. A nice young civil servant destined for the colonies has passed his final examination at Leyden University, with honours for Indonesian law and Arabic. While relaxing in his parental home in Amsterdam, he meets a nice young girl, tall and fair, who has just graduated in domestic economy. His father, a rather cynical surgeon, and his mother, a rather vague and distant person, approve of her, and they get on well with her parents. Her father is an over-worked but cheerful family doctor, her mother a homely, practical Amsterdam housewife. His father describes interesting cases in his clinic, hers tells about the troubles of his needy patients. Her mother

7

praises a new recipe for preserving vegetables, and his mother listens, polite but vague. He becomes engaged to Effie, marries her and takes her to Java.

He is posted as an Assistant District-officer in a nice small Javanese town. They are both new to the tropics, but they love the soft-spoken, polite natives. Every morning they have coffee on their lawn, and the dew is cool on their sandalled feet, and the gray doves are singing in their bamboo cages along the eaves of the white, rambling house behind them. The bicycle ride to the office is hot and dusty, but the work is full of varied interest, and one likes the work, and the people one has to work with. The night is cool again, and there are long talks in the intimacy of the shared mosquito-net, when Effie tells me, first shyly, then more frankly, about the simple, steady faith she has been raised in. She shows me the leather-bound volume she had kept hidden, shows it diffidently, because she has heard me refer to it once as mainly a source for historical research. Her father has written on the fly-leaf: "To our Eve, for her guidance and comfort." And I kiss her and I come very near to sharing her quiet assurance. The household runs smoothly under Effie's calm efficiency, she learns the language, carefully, from a small phrase-book she carries about in her key-basket, and the native servants listen to her, with respectful patience. Just when I am beginning to ask myself whether this friendly, placid existence is all that life has to offer, Effie becomes pregnant. When Bubu, our small girl, is born I recognize in her the sturdy small girl Effie must have been, with her finely spun golden hair and her large, serious blue eyes. Life seems full and good again, and I smother occasional nagging doubts with hard work. I often make extensive tours of inspection in my district, do much sociological research, and write up my data in the evening, working till deep in the night.   Finally I sum up my researches in my report "On the Suppression of Opium and Related Subjects" which is praised by the government in Batavia and often quoted, as the O.R.S. Report.   My colleagues predict a rapid promotion.   Then the headlines begin to talk about mounting tension in Europe, Holland is invaded and occupied, and Effie and I talk much about far-away Amsterdam, about our relatives and friends, and that brings us closer together again.   We hardly take notice of another war-threat, nearer to us, this time, yet so unreal.   And then the Japs are there.

I look up quickly, for I suddenly realize that I have been thinking aloud; as I am always doing when I reach this crucial point, on my bad days.   But I am in a rather quiet street now, and the few people that are about are hurrying along, each intent on his own particular business.   My business is to formulate my defense.   Even the prisoner in the dock is entitled to that.   He is entitled to explain extenuating circumstances — such as the utter confusion after the Jap landings, the desperate haste with which we tried to bolster up our pitifully inadequate defenses, the old-established relations with the natives that suddenly crumbled, the open destruction and the sneaking death in my district.   I had to rush around in my military jeep, deadly tired, my eyes inflamed by the smoke of the burning houses, my ears deafened by the roar of the planes.   And Lina is there, with her smouldering black eyes, and her cheek streaked with blood.   And then more blood, Effie's naked, mutilated body in a pool of blood that reeks with a raw smell.   And Bubu.   Of Bubu there is only her small curly head.

I halt and retch, violently.   Wiping my mouth with my handkerchief I see that I am all alone now in a deserted street. Beyond the sound of a motor-car somewhere behind me, all is

9

quiet. I am swaying on my feet, but I make it to the corner. As I round it a gust of ice-cold wind hits me full in the face. Automatically I press my chin on my breast. I must run, skip three squares of the pavement, four ... Then I see a small red square, directly in front of me. It is a red-leather wallet, shining red in the light of the street lamp. Just as I stoop to pick it up, a woman calls out, ahead. I quickly right myself, stuffing the wallet into the wide pocket of my mackintosh. Beyond the lamp-post I see two dark-faced men, one tall and one squat, in light-coloured trenchcoats. They are closing in on a woman in a dark-blue overcoat and a small red hat. She has just hit one with her large handbag, which has come open in her right hand. She raises her arm, but the tall man grabs it, and she cries out again.

Dark men coming out of the undergrowth, their white dresses very white in the glare of my headlamps. I swing the steering wheel of my jeep around, and the right fender crashes into the tree across the road. A shot rings out, then the burst of a Sten-gun. "Are you hurt, sir?" A wild, animal rage sears through my brain. I run towards them, grab the tall man by the lapels of his trenchcoat and floor him, as the army taught us. Then I turn to the squat one. But his right fist shoots out and I feel a hard blow on my jaw. The night is dark again.

"Are you hurt, sir?"

"No. Get that tree off the road, quick. I must ... " I break off, in utter confusion.

I am addressing a blue uniform, not the green one of our colonial army. An Amsterdam policeman is standing over me. And the small car behind him is white, not green. Green and blue and white merge, and I close my eyes.

Dazedly I try to figure out where I am. Then I understand. I am lying on the pavement, it presses up against my shoulder-blades, hard and cold. A muscular arm raises me to a sitting position, and I open my eyes. A little farther away stands another policeman, burly in his leather-jacket. He is talking to the girl with the red hat. While I am trying to bring these blurred images into focus I ask the policeman who is holding my shoulders:

"Where are those two fellows in trenchcoats? They ... they ... " I have seen the girl's face and stare at her in shocked astonishment.

"Got away, sir. But don't you worry, we'll get the scoundrels all right. The young miss has given us a good description, and my colleague has broadcast it already".

I want to nod, but a stinging pain shoots through my head, up from my throbbing jaw. It is nothing compared to the sickening pain that contracts my abdomen. For the girl has turned her head and the light of the street-lamp falls fully on her pale face now. It is Lina. Lina who is dead, but who has come back. Those are Lina's eyes, wide and black, and with the long lashes, the same oval face, the same full, slightly petulant mouth. I bury my face in my hands.

"Are you all right, sir?" the policeman asks solicitously. I raise my head and nod. He helps me to get on to my feet. As he gives me my hat he says: "Funny, we followed you for a while, because you were walking like a drunk."

"I wasn't feeling well. I get these sudden attacks of dizziness, sometimes."

"You weren't too dizzy to floor that scoundrel, though!" the policeman says cheerfully. I step up to the other. I must hear her voice.

"Janette Winter," the burly police officer says as he writes the name in his little book. The girl looks at me. Her face is taut, her eyes hostile. The resemblance to Lina is so close that it hurts. The officer asks her: "And you live in this pension here, eh? Abelstraat 55?"

She nods. I look away, down the deserted street. She is not the later Lina, her face distorted, her breast torn, a mass of blood. She is the young Lina I met that sultry night long before she died. I notice that the burly policeman is looking me over, critically.

"He isn't hurt?" he asks his thin colleague. When the other shakes his head, he goes on the girl: "Where do you work, miss?"

"I am a nurse". She mentions a well-known hospital. Yes, I knew she would have that deep voice with the rich timbre.

"You'll have to come to headquarters tomorrow morning, Miss Winter. We'll show you some photographs, perhaps the two fellows are there. We have quite a collection, you know. Ten o'clock suit you?"

She nods, pulling her dark-blue coat closer to her. The wind has died down, but there's frost in the still air. How long have I been unconscious? About ten minutes, I guess. The policeman says to me:

"Lucky you weren't hurt, sir. Those orientals often carry knives, you know. Could I have your name and address?"

I take my identity card from my breast pocket and hand it to him. It's simpler, that way. He reads out the details as he copies them in his notebook: Johan Hendriks, born Amsterdam March the 12th 1914, book-keeper at the Byenkorf. And my address, and the telephone number of the department store, and of my boarding-house. He returns the card to me and says:

"You'll be notified if we need your testimony."

"You came just at the right moment!" She says it to the three of us, together. Her lips smile, but there's a hard and wary glint in her large eyes. Then she looks me full into the face and adds, cordially: "Thank you very much, Mr. Hendriks."

She turns round to the door of No. 55. I read the lettering on the enamelled plate: "Pension Jansen". Underneath is a white bell button. Lifting her hand to press the button, she says over her shoulder to the two policemen and me:

"Thanks again, and goodnight!"

The loudspeaker in the police car begins to splutter and the burly officer jumps into the driver's seat. "Streetcar knocked over a man on Leidsestraat!" he snaps at his colleague.

"Could you give me a lift there?" I ask. Fingering my swollen jaw I add: "I do feel a bit shaky."

"Hop in," the thin one says. We get into the car and drive off.

The siren and the spluttering loudspeaker make conversation impossible, so I can concentrate on a small detail that is bothering me. Miss Winter didn't put her fore-finger on the bell button. She put it just beside it. I am far-sighted, and I saw it, clearly. Perhaps she missed it because she was nervous. She had just been assaulted, after all. It could also have been intentional, however. One never knows, with women like Lina. My head begins to throb, my thoughts are turning round again, too fast. I look up. We are at the first crossing of the Leidsestraat.

"Could you drop me here?" I ask.

The driver pulls up at the curb. His eyes are already on the crowd that is collecting ahead, round a halted streetcar.

13

The conductor is among them, he waves his arms, shouts explications. "Take it easy!" the thin policeman tells me. The car is off again.

A small group of people are standing on the corner, looking down the street at the halted streetcar.

"Walk smack into it, he did. Killed on the spot," a fat man in a heavy fur coat says. "Saw it myself." Then he adds, with dismay: "There wasn't much blood, though."

There isn't much blood, sometimes. Sometimes there is. I slip past them into the sidestreet, and enter the first café I see. I make my way through the crowded restaurant where the air is thick with tobacco smoke and the smell of coffee, to the quiet billiard room in the rear. The green cloth of the two billiard tables shines softly under the low-hanging, shaded lamps. Only one table is occupied, by two men in their shirt-sleeves. Apart from them there is no one about. I pull out a chair in the dark corner by the cue-rack, and lay my wet hat on the chair opposite. The room is heated well but I don't take off my mackintosh, for I feel really dizzy now, and I am swaying on my feet. I sit down with a sigh of satisfaction.

The rotund billiard player with the chubby face mutters a curse at a near miss. He sets his cue down hard and calls out to me:

"What was the siren for? Accident?"

"Yes," I say, "there was an accident, down the street. But I didn't see it."

There had indeed been an accident, on that crucial night. And that accident I did see, right before my eyes. I was sitting in the ill-lit, stifling hot bar room of the dingy small hotel, in a Bandong suburb. I am dog-tired, my uniform jacket is sticking to my aching, wet back. The wall clock says it is a quarter past ten. The Malay bartender looks bored, even the occasional roar of a Japanese plane overhead doesn't seem to interest him. I am having a tepid beer before I set out in my jeep again. An hour's drive through the dark countryside will take me home. Bubu will be asleep, of course, and Effie too. Effie must have had a gruelling day also, for she is with a mobile Redcross unit.

A volley of shots resounds in the distance, somewhere behind the hotel. I ask the bartender for ice. He shrugs his shoulders. I should have known. The ice-factory got a direct hit, that morning. Suddenly there are shouts outside. The screen door is flung open and a woman comes rushing inside, her long raven-black hair fluttering about her head. She stumbles on her high heels and falls down between two chairs, by the door. While she is trying frantically to get up, a soldier bursts inside, bare-headed, his tunic open in front. Blood gushes down his distorted face, from a gaping wound in his forehead. He grabs the woman's arm and raises his curved sabre to cleave her head. By then I have my service pistol out and I shoot. The force of the bullet smacks his back against the doorpost. As he sinks to the floor, two white-helmeted military policemen come in. They quickly survey the situation, then they salute and tell me that the soldier got into a drunken street brawl with two others, over the woman. He was knocked down, and hit his head on the edge of the curb. When he got up, he was raving mad. He emptied his pistol into his two friends, then went after the woman with his sabre. There's no need for long explanations or for filling out official papers. Things like this are happening all the time, all over the town. The two men carry the dead soldier off, and I help the woman to get up. I make her sit in a chair, and order a brandy for her from the bartender, who has come out again from under the counter.

She is young and beautiful. Evidently she has Indonesian blood, but she is white, a creamy white, as some of them are. She has a magnificent figure, her white satin brassière and white satin pants shine through the thin fabric of her flowered muslin dress. Looking up at me with her large, flashing eyes she dabs the bleeding scratch on her cheek with a small lace handkerchief.

She reads the look in my eyes with practised ease. She tells me that she is called Lina, and that she has a room, in that same small hotel. All the accumulated tension, the frustrated rage of the last twenty-four sleepless hours concentrate into an urgent, burning desire for this woman. As we go upstairs she remarks, casually:

"I must warn you that I am tired. You may not get your due."

Yes, that was Lina. Casual. And the girl in the street just now was casual. Suddenly my head feels like an empty dome that grows wider, higher. I quickly bend my head down towards my knees and just manage not to pass out. My swollen jaw stings. The waiter appears, and the billiard players order a beer. I order a black coffee and, as an afterthought, a platter of ham sandwiches. I light a cigarette and draw on it, eagerly inhaling the smoke. Perhaps that will settle my stomach.

Two days later Effie is dead, and Bubu is dead. Have they been buried? Probably not. I am in the prison camp. Lina has not been interned, because she claims she is half-Indonesian. She gives me my due, and to spare. For she visits me regularly, smuggles Japanese cigarettes in for me, and vitamin

16

tablets, and medicine. And I need those. For I am beaten up, and interrogated under torture again and again, through one of those silly mistakes that cost many a man his life, in those days. Hendriks is a common name, and the Japanese military police were convinced I was another Hendriks, one of our intelligence-agents who had caused them a lot of trouble. They wanted me to tell them the names and whereabouts of the other agents hiding in that area. I could quite see their point. However, although I had been made a captain overnight, I hadn't had anything to do with intelligence, and I simply didn't know the answers. Sometimes, when I couldn't stand the torture any longer, I just made up the answers. That meant a reprieve of a few weeks, for they checked up all my stories, meticulously. And then they tortured me again. But I survived. When the war was over, Lina was waiting for me at the camp gate, with a carton of cigarettes. British, this time. I married her, got sick-leave and took her to Holland. After two months in Amsterdam I signed up as a circuit judge, and we went back to Java.

The waiter puts the coffee and the platter of sandwiches at my elbow. I gulp down the hot coffee. Then I start on the sandwiches and watch the billiard game. It has a soothing effect, for the two men play seriously and very well. Especially the chubby one, who has a beautiful smooth stroke. His large round head with the slightly protruding eyes keeps bobbing up and down above the green cloth as he carefully builds up his long breaks, oblivious of his surroundings. It reminds me of the head of a goldfish, bobbing up and down among the green water plants in its own small world of glass.

I must also concentrate — and decide which was greater, my love or my hate. I loved Lina because of her uncontrolled, spasmodic passion for me, for the almost animal ferocity of her fighting surrender; for her exuberant joy of living, and for her pathetic, often nearly childlike, simplicity. I hated her for her frequent spells of vicious temper that goaded me into outbursts of degrading rage, and I hated her for the pangs of unreasonable, debasing jealousy she caused me. And also, incongruously, for her part in the murder of Effie and Bubu. The servants feared and despised Lina, they considered her as one of their own, despite her white skin. In her generous moods she would heap presents on them, at other times she would spoil for trouble, lashing them with her tongue, humiliating them, especially Amat, our good-looking houseboy. But I must not run ahead of events. I must get everything in the right chronological order; that is important. There came another war, a strange unreal war that was called a police-action. The nationalist rebels are here and everywhere, the Dutch administration is crumbling away. Old feuds flare up. Old scores are settled, by a quick knife-thrust in the dark, by a single shot that rings out from an empty house. The tense atmosphere of constant danger makes me irritable. But Lina gets very quiet, she withdraws into a shell of fear. When she tells me that she is with child, she does so in a sullen manner, nearly hostile. And she makes scenes with the servants, disgusting, nerve-racking scenes. But when I tell her she must go to a safe place, to the hospital in Surabaya, she refuses to budge from my side, passionately. And I love her as never before.

Soon after, the end. I must be very careful now, for now every moment, literally every second counts. I must concentrate. I lean back in my chair, and thrust my hands deep into the pockets of my mackintosh. The waiter flits past, and I order a second cup of coffee. Suddenly the fingers of my right hand close around a soft leather object. I take out a small red-morocco wallet.

I am looking at it as it lies in my palm, astonished. Suddenly I remember. That is the wallet I picked up from the pavement, just before I saw Janette Winter. Janette Winter in her dark-blue coat and her red hat, attacked by two dark men in light trenchcoats.

I can't open the wallet. Lina is still too close. I never opened Lina's handbag or wallet. It would have been an unspeakable, vile intrusion on her feminine privacy, as unthinkable as watching her at moments when one doesn't watch a woman, not even one's own wife. Strange, with Effie it was different. Effie's bag and wallet I would open as a matter of course; every time I needed a key, or small change, and whether she was present or not. I didn't even stop to think about it. Nor did Effie.

I take hold of myself. This is not the confused, threatening past. This is the straight and simple, the saving present. I have to open this wallet and inspect its content, because I must verify whether it really belongs to Miss Winter. It may have been dropped by a passer-by. And it may have been flung out of Miss Winter's handbag when she hit out with it at the tall man who was attacking her. This wallet must be returned to its rightful owner. Simple and logical. The present will save me.

I find three bills of ten guilders each, and an identity-card. I put on my reading glasses. First I examine the photograph. I see to my surprise that it is an excellent likeness, evidently an expensive studio portrait. Yes, Lina would never have cheap snap-shots, not even for her passport. I read the neat block-writing, and all of a sudden my newly-acquired composure is lost. "Eveline Vanhagen, born June the 3rd 1940. Profession: Artiste. Address: Oudegracht 88."

So she tells lies as easily, as naturally as Lina did. The block writing on the card becomes blurred, as everything became blurred that hot oppressive afternoon when Lina told me her last lie. But was it a lie? Neither of us had slept during the siesta, stretched out apathetically on the clammy sheets, drenched with our perspiration. Lina had tried to goad me into a quarrel, as she would often do, when she was restive and afraid. My nerves were as taut as violin strings, but I had not reacted. I was too tired, after the long morning in the hot courtroom. When we had taken our shower, and were listlessly dressing for the afternoon tea, she suddenly told me, casually, that the child she was expecting wasn't mine. The blow came so sudden that it stunned me completely. I did not say a word. My silence seemed to disappoint her, for I noticed that she eyed me furtively, in the mirror before which she was doing up her hair.

Silently we went to the front verandah and sat down in the rattan chairs, overlooking the garden. Automatically I put my service pistol on the table, beside my tea cup, as we were instructed to do. For there had been rebel infiltrations in our district, and the day before our military commander had been wounded by a sniper. Our quiet Javanese servant, who had come when Amat was dismissed, places the silver platter with cakes in front of Lina, then he disappears. Now I must get everything very clear, for every second counts. Lina takes a small cake and leans back in her chair, nibbling at it with a contented air. I can't stand that secretive, self-satisfied smile, just after she has told me, and I avert my eyes, to the garden. The low flowering shrubs seem to quiver, because of the hot, moist air that hangs over them. I was staring at the hedge, but I did not really see it. I may have vaguely associated a few brown leaves with Amat's face, because in that split second it flashed through my mind that she might have lied just to goad me, as she was wont to goad Amat by telling lies about him to the other servants. And I may have actually thought that the thing that suddenly stuck out of the foliage was a dead branch. But I can't swear to it. Then, there's another point. Suppose I had consciously seen the flash of Amat's face, and recognised the dead branch for what it really was, would I have had sufficient time to grab my pistol, aim and shoot? I am a good marksman, but was there sufficient time? I have reconstructed the scene uncounted times, but this always remains a debatable point. Only two hard facts stand out clearly. That for one brief moment I wished she were dead, and that the rifle bullet hit her full in the breast. She died in my arms.

I look dazedly at the sheet of paper in my trembling hands. With an effort I bring it into focus, and I see the heading, clumsily printed with a toy printing-set: Bert Winter, Oude-gracht 88. And thereunder, in a neat, print-like hand: Dearest Eveline. Without realizing it I must have unfolded the piece of cheap notepaper that was in the wallet. I clutch at the present, the safe present, and I read on.

> *You know how I hate to bother you, and I am awfully sorry to bother you now. Especially since only yesterday I told you that I understood, and that I didn't mind your accepting the offer. But now, after one day and one night without you, I feel I must make a last attempt. And therefore I say: don't go. Please!*
>
> *Yours, Bert*

Suddenly I am shocked at myself. I shouldn't have read that note, of course. Automatically I look at the date, scribbled in the lower left corner: February the 26th. The day before yesterday. I take off my reading glasses and put the case in my breast pocket. Well, I have read the letter, that can't be helped. And I want to think about Bert Winter, and about Eveline: about the day before yesterday, not about that day in the hot, sultry garden, long ago.

Bert Winter is a man Eveline is living with, on Oudegracht 88. Has been living with, that is, for she has left. Lina didn't leave me, that I have to admit. I left her.

"Fine massé shot!" the chubby billiard player shouts. He is watching intently his opponent, who is nursing the three balls along the cushion with impressive precision. I used to be good at that too. I love precise, controlled action, and the precise reasoning based on hard facts that one uses in court. Eveline is a fact, very real, a girl in a dark-blue coat and a red hat. Her lover is a shadowy person, as yet. Let me try to bring him into focus by reasoning. He is an educated man, judging by his unadorned, intellectual handwriting and his adult, controlled style. Probably he wears spectacles for near-sightedness, for his writing has a kind of print-like precision. He can't be too well off, for he had to use for this important letter a sheet torn from a cheap blocknote, and Eveline's coat didn't seem too new, now that I come to think about it. Bert's style is adult, but he must still be a bit boyish, in some ways. For there's the clumsy letterhead — an attempt at establishing an identity, at low cost. Eveline left him, but not for Pension Jansen, Abelstraat 55. Of that I am sure.

I call the waiter, too loud. The billiard player miscues, and his chubby opponent gives me a reproachful look. Feeling genuinely sorry, I over-tip the waiter, and I leave.

A teeming, noisy evening crowd is about in the street. Every one of those people must have a purpose. I have a purpose too now. I make for the taxi stand on the corner.

"Oudegracht 88, please" I tell the driver.

He starts up the motor and deftly joins the traffic stream. He drives very well indeed and I sit back and enjoy watching him at it. I love precise, manual skill. That's why I love billiards, and line drawing, and target practice. I love also mental precision: cold, intellectual reasoning, impersonal. That's why I took the job of book-keeper which I don't need, for my pension is sufficient for my modest livelihood. My emotional life is so hopelessly tangled up that I must grope for concrete things I can clutch at in order to steady myself. This is reflected also in my reluctance to part from an old, worn-down car, from an old pistol, from a worn suit or hat. For these old, thoroughly familiar objects help me, by giving me some of the support I so desperately need. Is it for the same reason that I shrink from putting an end to my own shadowy existence, as I have thought of doing, occasionally, during the last years in my boarding house, here in Amsterdam? Because I fear that if I should lose my body, I shall also lose . . . ? Mechanically I feel in my sidepocket. The tin tube is still there. Has been there, ever since I got it from my friend the army surgeon, when the Japs came nearer and nearer. "Be careful with those tablets," he said. "One will still pain, two ensure peaceful sleep. The rest will make you sleep so soundly that you'll never wake up." He died somewhere in the jungle, from starvation, they say. I often wonder whether he himself kept a tube of those tablets with him.

The picturesque cursing of my driver makes me come back to the present. We are advancing slowly along a narrow canal-street. Two cars could hardly pass each other in the cobbled space left between the high, irregular graystone curb and the unprotected edge of the dark canal. A little farther on stands a black delivery van, several feet from the water edge.

"There's your number 88," the driver mutters. Looking at me over his shoulder he adds: "I'll have to back up all the way to the corner again. See that van some blasted fool left standing there?" He drives off, changing his gears noisily, despite the tip I gave him.

I am in one of the oldest parts of the city, near the Amstel. The grimy, gable-roofed houses are dark, the only light comes from the row of old-fashioned iron lamp-posts, at regular intervals along the edge of the canal. No. 86 is an old-style pharmacy. Over the door hangs the wooden head of a turbaned Turk, his wide open mouth displays a long, red tongue. It is a so-called gaper, the traditional pharmacist's shop-sign, but it vaguely disturbs me. The wide black eyes seem to fix me with an obscene leer. I quickly climb the five stone steps that lead up to the high door of No. 88. The green paint is flaking away all around the brass knocker that has the shape of a lion's head. I take out my cigarette lighter and scan the names of the inhabitants, under the bell button in the doorpost. On the first floor is Nivas Ltd., im- and export. That is a familiar name, there was a large organization of the sugar industry of that name, in Java. On the second floor lives a gentleman's tailor and a painter. On the third, three students of chemistry. Their names are scribbled on smudged visiting cards. None of them is called Bert Winter. I turn round and stare at the dark canal. A small motorboat of the Water Police comes chug-chugging down the Amstel. Its eerie roof-light reminds me of Charon's ferry. Is this excursion into the present leading to a dead end? With a sudden pang of anxiety I realize how tenuous the link is. Then it flashes through my mind that there must be a basement.

I quickly descend into the street again. Yes, underneath the stone stairs a narrow flight of steps leads down to a brown door. I eagerly squint at the printed card stuck behind the glass of the peephole. It says: Bert Winter, Bachelor of Law. That fits with my mental picture of Bert. A student. I glance at the two windows, half below street level. Under the heavy drapes there's a strip of light. I press the bell button, firmly.

The door opens nearly at once. Mr. Winter has evidently heard the taxi and he was waiting behind the door. He's expecting a caller.

He is taller than I, broad in the shoulders, narrow waist. He has rather long, curly hair, but I can't make out his face, for the bare bulb of the hall light he switches on is very strong.

"Yes?" he asks in a pleasant voice.

"My name is Hendriks," I inform him politely. "I have something for Miss Vanhagen. For Eveline. And I..."

"Come inside," he interrupts me brusquely. He doesn't ask me to take off my coat but opens the door on his left and ushers me into a low-ceilinged, untidy room. It is lit by· a desk-lamp with a green shade which stands on a table littered with books and papers. Although it's a typical cheap rented room, it is nice and warm. The old-fashioned pot-bellied coal-stove in front of the chimney is glowing red.

"Sit down!" my host says. He points at the straw-bottomed kitchen chair that stands by the desk. He ignores the old upholstered armchair behind it, pushes a pile of fat law-books aside and sits half on the edge of the desk, his feet planted on the threadbare carpet. Evidently he wants the interview to be brief.

He moved with the lithe grace of the trained athlete, and his tailored brown tweedsuit accentuates his muscular build. He is older than I had expected, about thirty, I would say. He has a regular, handsome face with a small fair moustache and a wide, rather humorous mouth. His curly fair hair is neatly parted on one side. Carefully arranging the faultless crease of his trousers, his porcelain-blue, level eyes give me an appraising look. I notice the heavy pouches under his eyes. Perhaps it is those that make him appear older than he is.

I want to place my hat on the pile of student notebooks on the desk, but check myself when I realize that the hat is still wet, and I put it on the floor. The notebook that is lying open on top of the pile is heavily scored in red; the hand-writing of the red remarks matches that of Bert's letter to Eveline. Bert is making some extra money by correcting the work of younger students. I did so myself, a long time ago. And Bert needs extra money, for there isn't a single piece of good furniture in the room. An untidily made-up day-bed, a stand with a cooking plate in the corner, a rickety set of bookshelves stacked with pocket editions, that is all. On the wall are two reproductions of Gauguin, torn from an illustrated weekly, and two large coloured photographs of cinema stars. And another one of a ballet girl, in an alluring pose. The photographs are Eveline's contribution, I presume.

"Thank you, yes," I say to my host, who is offering me his open cigarette-case. It's a good Egyptian import-brand. As he takes one himself I notice that his fingertips are stained by nicotine. He is an athlete, but out of training. He waits till I have lit my cigarette, then he says casually:

"Miss Vanhagen isn't here, you know."

"Oh, she'll be working, of course!" I say with a fatuous grin. "She told me the name of the place. I had better go there and ... "

I half-rise. The tricks of the circuit judge's trade come back to me, almost automatically.

"No," he says impatiently, "She isn't at Chez Claude. She's taking a holiday."

"I didn't know that," I say ruefully as I resume my seat. "Ought to have written first, of course. I am living in The Hague, you see. Lost contact, more or less. My own fault. When will she be back?"

"In two weeks or so. But I'd write her a card first, to make sure, if I were you, Mr. Hendriks."

He speaks with a slight accent. His rolling r has an American flavour.

"Yes," I say, "I'll do that. Where ... ?" I look around for an ash tray.

He scans the desk, then jumps down and walks over to the chimney, with quick, sure strides. He comes back with a saucer and puts it on the desk. Resuming his perch there he says:

"Sorry. Don't know what happened to my ashtrays. That damned charwoman ... " He pauses, and studies the tip of his cigarette. Then he asks, very casually: " Have you known Miss Vanhagen for a long time, Mr. Hendriks?"

"Well, I have been abroad for a while, you know, rather neglected her, I must confess. I saw a lot of her two years ago. We took lessons together, as a matter of fact. A bit of elocution, a bit of acting, that kind of thing."

"Are you also in the show-business?" he asks, incredulously. I don't blame him, I hardly look like a nightclub entertainer. I say hastily:

"No, I am a lawyer, I work for an insurance company. But I am interested in the show business. As a hobby."

He relaxes and asks with an encouraging smile:

"Financially interested, eh?"

"Oh no. I like the atmosphere, you know. Always enjoy associating with artists. Takes one out of oneself, if you know what I mean."

He knows it all right. I am the well-to-do chap who gives the girls a good time, after the show. Champagne with the supper, and a hotel room with bath. He gets on to his feet and says:

"Well, I am sorry that Eveline isn't here. Want to leave a message?"

"Just tell her that I'll write to her, Mr. Winter."

"I'll do that."

I would like to prolong the interview, but I can't think of a good leading question. I point at the pile of law books.

"Rather a bore when you have to memorize all those" I remark. "But I found out that they are useful, later."

"Very useful," he agrees. His nose points at the door.

I get up and we go out into the hall.

"Sorry to have bothered you," I say.

"Not at all." He opens the door. It is raining again.

"Beastly weather," he says.

"Awful." We don't shake hands.

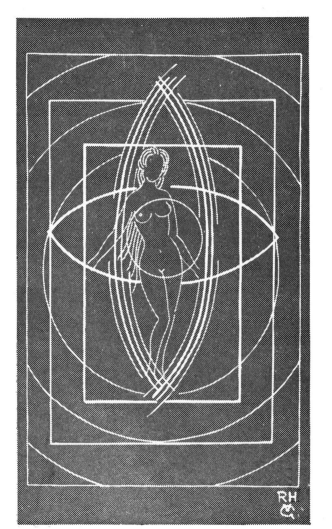

THROUGH A VEIL OF GLASS

I put the collar of my mackintosh up, for the wind is rising again and sudden gusts drive the rain into my neck. I see that the delivery van is still there. It looks rather old, and the number-plate is covered with mud. I walk down the street the way the taxi came.

In the next street there are many small shops, and more people are about. Sauntering along I try to put the finishing touches to my mental picture of Eveline Vanhagen and Bert Winter. Since Eveline works at Chez Claude, the term "artiste" on her identity card means she is one of the many third-rate singers and dancers who appear for a few minutes on the miniature stage of that large, noisy dancing-hall, every-time the jazz orchestra needs a break for a smoke and a beer. The management proudly announces these performances as a floorshow, but the couples who visit this popular dancing come to dance and to look at each other, not at a show. As to Bert, he is a slightly untidy but serious youngster. He doesn't smoke, either because he doesn't like it, or in order to save money. But there's a romantic streak in him, hence his liaison with an "artiste", and the Gauguin reproductions. But where is he? And where is Eveline?

The problem fascinates me, because it links me firmly with the present. And also because of a vague feeling that Eveline may help me to find the answers to some of the questions that are rising up from the past. If I can find her, at least.

As to the man who acted as my kind host just now, about him I have no doubts at all. That expensively dressed, well cared for gentleman who smokes Egyptian cigarettes was entirely out of place in that poor student's room. He was a visitor, just like me. He evidently is a plain-clothes policeman. I nearly collide with a police officer, one in full uniform. I apologize and ask politely how I get to Abelstraat. He consults his city-plan and tells me that the streetcar on the next crossing will take me to that neighbourhood.

The streetcar is packed with noisy humanity. The smell of damp clothes and stale perspiration is mixed with cheap perfume. As a rule I hate crowded places for they make me feel acutely miserable. But now the people don't bother me at all. I listen with interest to fragments of conversation, and I laugh at a joke of the conductor's.

After I have alighted from the streetcar, a short walk takes me to Abelstraat. I halt on the corner to orientate myself. Two men carrying wet umbrellas brush past me, a cyclist comes from the other direction, pedalling furiously. A few private cars come gliding past, slowly, because of the rain. No police car is parked in the vicinity of Pension Jansen, no one seems to be loitering about there. The police are interested only in Oudegracht 88. As yet.

As I walk down the street I study the stately houses that line it on both sides. They are solidly constructed, and nearly all of them have four floors. These houses date from the early years of the century, and were built by well-to-do people for their own use; people who could afford two maids, sleeping in. The nameplates prove that now most houses have been divided up into three or four separate flats, or have been turned into offices of business organizations. I cross over to the graystone building that is directly opposite Pension Jansen. The large bronze doorplate states that it is one of the offices of the Municipal Council. Perhaps it is the place where the owner of the tweed-elbow of Jan's pub earns his salary. Jan's pub can't be far away. Or is it? I didn't pay any attention to where I went, after I had left there.

A few of the windows of Pension Jansen are lit, and also some of No. 57, its architectural twin. No. 53 is completely dark. The two windows of the ground floor have no curtains. There's a white strip of paper stuck across them, with the word "Sold" on it, in large letters. I throw my cigarette away, cross the street, and press the bell button of Pension Jansen.

An elderly woman in a neat black dress opens. She eyes me rather dubiously. I take off my hat and say politely:

"Miss Winter told me that she had moved here, madam. I would like to ..."

"There's no Miss Winter staying here," the old lady interrupts me sourly. "I don't take single young women. Only married couples."

It's a wise policy, I admit, but it doesn't get me anywhere. I resume, somewhat diffidently:

"Perhaps she meant the house next door then, for ..."

"Nonsense. Fifty-seven is a home for aged persons, and fifty-three has been standing empty these last three months. A shame, I call it, the housing shortage being what it is." She begins to close the door.

"Did you see the accident?" I ask quickly.

The door is wide open again.

"Accident? Here in the street?" she asks eagerly. "Did it happen just now?"

"No, about an hour ago, they said. Good-bye!"

It is I who pull the door shut. I need not try No. 51, for it is an institute for industrial research. I ring at the door of No. 57, the home for aged persons. The doorman recognizes me. When he heard people talk in the street, he had looked through the window and seen me, Eveline and the two policemen. He had drawn the curtain shut again when he saw that all the excitement was over, just before the police car left. Therefore he can't say where Eveline went. No. 53, the empty house, is my last chance. I am certain she has slipped into a house close by Pension Jansen. She couldn't have risked crossing or walking down the street while I was driving off with the two policemen, for one of us might have looked round and seen her. I walk over to the municipal building again, and survey No. 53

The rain has changed into a drizzle, so that now I get a better view of the house. It has only three floors, but there's an air of subdued opulence about it. The high door is decorated with sculpted scrolls, and over it is an old-fashioned awning of coloured glass. The pointed slate-roof is topped by a weather-vane of wrought iron. I peer intently at the three small windows directly under the roof. There's a faint glow of light behind the yellow roll-curtain of the one in the middle. Why should there be a light in a house that has been standing empty for three months? A caretaker, perhaps? I'll look into this anyway, for it is my last chance of maintaining the link with the present. But I'll approach the house from the back. There's more traffic in the street now, and I have made myself too conspicuous already. I go to the next street that runs parallel with Abelstraat. Hurriedly, for the standing about has made my feet ice-cold.

I am looking for one of those narrow passages in between two houses that lead to the alley along their backgardens. The first two are barred, but the third is open. When I am in the alley, littered with refuse, I easily locate the back of No. 53, because it's the only house of three storeys, and because of the weather-vane. A light is burning behind the curtained French windows of the second floor. That eliminates the theory about the caretaker. There are people living in this empty house.

A broad balcony runs along the entire width of the second floor. The balcony of the third floor is narrow, and the two windows up there are dark. I scan the backs of the other houses. Most windows are lighted, some people haven't even drawn the curtains close. I can see them, but they can't see me, down below between the dark garden walls.

I try the green garden door. It is bolted on the inside. Fortunately the top of the garden wall is not protected by glass shards. I reach up and climb over it. This No. 53 hasn't much of a garden, it's just a patch of gravel surrounded by a neglected grass border. In the corner on my right, half under the balcony, is a toolshed. An old oil drum is lying in front of it. I set the drum upright, step on to it, and on the roof of the tool-shed; from there the balcony is within easy reach. When I have stepped over the iron railing, I anxiously inspect the row of houses opposite. But no window is thrown open and there's no indignant outcry. I carefully tread over the wet boards, up to the slit in the red-plush curtains that hang in multiple folds behind the glass pane of the nearest French window. My face close to the glass, I peer inside.

What I see is an anti-climax: a large man slumped in an armchair, and plainly bored. He has unbuttoned the upper part of the waistcoat of his gray striped suit, and pushed his bowler-hat far back from his broad, smooth brow. His hands are folded in his lap, his long legs stretched out towards the large electric heater. The heater is burning high, and it's a brand-new one, for its cardboard box is standing beside it. The box serves as a table; on it is a glass ashtray, and a small portable radio. These modern appliances contrast sharply with the old-fashioned high chimney of carved red marble, supported by two naked Greek ladies, of white marble. Their obvious charms do not interest the large man. His heavy-jowled, sallow face is expressionless, his drooping eyelids half closed. The long cigar between his thick lips isn't burning. He looks bored. Utterly bored.

On the other side of the heater stands an empty wooden crate. There's no other furniture, at least none that I can see. The pink wall paper has a flower design in gold, but it is badly stained. Dark squares indicate the places where pictures hung, once; they stress the atmosphere of faded gentility. The floor-covering has been taken up, so that the bare wooden boards show. I reflect that the glaring light must come from a strong lamp in the other half of the room, beyond my range of vision. Perhaps it comes from a large crystal chandelier, as one expects in an old-style room like this.

The man is too well dressed for a caretaker. He must be the owner, who has decided to camp in his newly-acquired house, pending the arrival of the furniture. Or of his wife, for I notice he wears a broad golden wedding ring on his pudgy hand. Whatever he is, he has a right to be there, and be bored. I had better go back the way I came. With a red morocco wallet I can't deliver.

Suddenly a guttural voice speaks up, somewhere above me. I press myself close to the wall. I have been discovered, by someone on the receding balcony of the floor above. I wait, holding my breath. But nothing happens. Again I hear the voice. I look up, and heave a sigh of relief. The flapwindow of the transom over the French window at the other end of the balcony is open. I tiptoe up to the high window underneath. There the plush curtains are a few inches apart. Now I can see the entire large room. And I feel a glow of satisfaction.

In the glare of the strong unshaded electric bulb that hangs in the centre of the bare, empty room I see two men sitting on the old upholstered sofa, on my right. Between them and the large man by the electric heater there's only a long, broad stretch of bare, scarred floor boards. In the wall opposite me are two doors, painted a cream white, with gilded borders. The two men on the sofa wear neat, dark-blue suits, and maroon ties. They are the two dark-faced men who assaulted Eveline in the street.

The smaller one shrugs his padded shoulders.

"It can't be helped," he says sullenly. "Why don't we go out, for a while?"

It's Arabic, and the Arabic spoken in Egypt. I am more familiar with the Arabic of Hadramaut, as spoken by the Arab merchants on Java. But I spent a summer vacation in Egypt when I was a student in Leyden, and I think I'll manage.

The small man is sitting hunched forward, his elbows on his knees. He has a very dark, smooth face with broad cheekbones and a narrow, pointed chin. His eyes are large, his mouth small but very red. His blue-black hair falls in oily curls over his low wrinkled brow. His coat is narrow in the waist, his trousers are faultlessly creased, but his brown shoes are too light, nearly yellow. He is about twenty-five, and he is the fellow who knocked me down.

The other, who was floored by me, is tall and spare. He leans back in his corner of the sofa, his long legs crossed, his arms folded across his breast. He has a lean, regular face, not as dark as that of his companion, with a small moustache, and marked by a prominent aquiline nose. He is older than the other, about forty, I think. He is staring at the bored man by the electric heater with a far-away look, the desert-dweller's look. He is indeed an Egyptian of the Bedouin type — and a handsome specimen of the type, I must admit. The small man repeats impatiently:

"Couldn't we go out again, eh? See something of the town?"

The tall man slowly turns round at him and says coldly:

"You are nervous, Mochtar. Yet you were not nervous in France. Neither in Italy, or in Germany."

The other looks even more sullen. His large eyes shine as if they were wet. Puckering his small red mouth he says:

"I hate waiting, Achmad. Especially in this damned cold and wet town." Pointing with his chin at the other end of the room he adds: "Its all the fault of that fat fool over there, the stupid son of a dog."

"It's Figel's mistake all right," Achmad admits. "He was told that the Djibouty would sail for Alexandria on the last day of this month, and Figel thought it meant she would sail today. Since, however, this month happens to have twenty-nine days this year, the Djibouty will sail tomorrow. We can do nothing but wait."

He speaks Arabic beautifully, with the careful pronunciation of a man who is familiar with the classical language, and loves it. His cultivated language contrasts sharply with the slip-shod, vulgar dialect used by his companion. I feel like a spectator in a theatre, on a front seat. The large, brilliantly lit scene is cleverly set: the large man in front of the heater on the extreme left, two men on a sofa on the extreme right, and the centre empty, ready for the appearance of the main actor — if any. I need not consult my program to know their names: the large man with the bowler-hat is called Figel, the tall Egyptian Achmad, the small one Mochtar. There's a long silence, and I close my eyes. For some people feel an unseen person watching them. Suddenly Mochtar speaks up again:

"Let's go out and have a look around."

Achmad crushes his cigarette in the glass ash-tray standing between them. He has smoked only half of it. He says haughtily:

"I know what you mean by looking around, Mochtar. And I tell you it is dangerous. This house belongs to Figel, it is uncomfortable, but it is safe. You are a stranger here, and you speak only broken English. Who knows what you will say to the scum you like to associate with? Who knows what they will say, to others?"

There is no answer. I look inside again. Mochtar's red mouth is distorted in a sneer, and there's a vicious glint in his large eyes. The other doesn't notice that, he is staring straight ahead again. Then he resumes, in the same measured voice:

"We must be here when Meekhaeel returns. I want to be sure there are no complications. The Sheikh does not want complications."

Mochtar lights a cigarette with quick, nervous gestures.

"We shouldn't have spent so much time on that side-issue," he snaps. "That kind of merchandise is readily available. Anywhere."

"Not to Figel, apparently."

Silence again.

I wonder whom Achmad was referring to. The name Michael is familiar to Arabs from their religious books. But Moslems don't use it as personal name. Only Christian Arabs, such as those in Lebanon. I cast a quick look at the house fronts behind me, and promptly a stream of cold water leaks into my collar. The steady drizzle is drenching my hat and my mackintosh.

"You who speak many tongues," Mochtar resumes, "you ask that fat dog at what time the Djibouty will sail tomorrow." He pauses before adding casually: "Ask him also why we aren't going back by plane. We went to Italy by plane, and to Germany. Why return home by boat?"

Achmad gives him a long appraising look. As the small man averts his eyes, Achmad speaks:

"I shall transmit to Figel your first question, Mochtar, not the second. For your second question is irrelevant, and one does not question the orders of the Sheikh." He calls over at the bored man, in correct English: "When is the Djibouty sailing tomorrow, Mr. Figel?"

"Eh?" The large man gives him a sour look. "At what time? At ten in the morning. We shall leave here at nine, because it is a long way, to the Levant Quay." He speaks with a pronounced German accent. He takes out a box of matches, and now at last relights his long cigar.

"You heard him," Achmad tells Mochtar placidly. "When is our coffee coming?"

"The dancer is asleep of course, the lazy slut! Why did Figel take her? Does she know about the other merchandise?"

"Of course not. You are nervous, Mochtar." He takes a gold-plated cigarette-case from his waistcoat pocket with slow, deliberate movements. As he carefully selects a cigarette, he says to the other, without looking at him:

"This morning you made an unseemly remark, Mochtar. You said that my wife is beautiful. And you said the same thing three days ago, in Hamburg, when we were collecting the last of our merchandise. Now you are a guttersnipe raised in the slums of Port Said, Mochtar, but you may have heard it said that Arab gentlemen do not refer to each other's wives, let alone pass remarks upon their looks. Since both of us are

40

living in the Sheikh's residence, it can't be avoided that you catch a glimpse of my wife, now and then. But you shall refrain from passing remarks on her."

Achmad lights his cigarette with a golden lighter, and puffs out the smoke in perfect circles.

Mochtar's large eyes seem to grow larger still, the white shows in startling contrast with his dark skin. He wants to say something but he checks himself and quickly looks round at the nearest door. My host of Oudegracht 88 comes inside.

I feel a thrill of excitement. Now the fat is in the fire! But I am disappointed. He just waves his hand at the two Egyptians on the sofa, then he takes off his heavy brown overcoat and hangs it on a nail in the door. He wants to put there his brown felt hat too, but thinks better of it when he sees it is dripping wet. He takes it with him, over to Figel, and lays it on the floor, in front of the electric heater. He remains standing there, warming his legs. Figel looks up and remarks:

"You were a long time. Find anything?"

"Nothing. And I had a good look, I tell you. Just when I was going to leave I was interrupted by some fool, a former beau of hers. I got rid of him as fast as I could. That old van of yours stinks, Figel. I had bad trouble with the starter."

He speaks English fluently, and I now place his accent. It is definitely American.

"You fixed the starter yourself, Miguel?" Figel asks, worriedly.

"Of course."

Figel nods. Miguel calls out to the two men on the sofa: "There was nothing." He lights a cigarette and asks Figel, casually: "Got anything out of the boy?"

"No. I told you she doesn't talk, didn't I? Not even to that fool of a boy-friend." There's an edge to Figel's voice.

Extravagant images flash through my mind. Eveline and Bert are kept imprisoned here, victims of this bunch of international crooks. I must help them escape, I shall ...

The second door opens and Eveline comes inside, carrying a tray. She deftly kicks the door shut with her slippered foot, then crosses the room to Figel and Miguel. She places the tray on the cardboard box. Miguel makes room for her in front of the stove, and she goes to stand there, her hands thrust into the pockets of the high-collared maroon housecoat she is wearing. Figel reaches out and takes a coffee cup from the tray. Miguel follows his example. I take note automatically that there are two cups left on the tray.

I am stunned, completely. Dazedly I watch Eveline as she bends over the radio and turns on a soft jazz music. Miguel offers her a cigarette and lights it for her. Suddenly I realize that I have pressed my face close to the window pane and that anyone looking this way will see me. I step aside, turn round and lean my back against the brick wall by the window. My legs are shaking.

She was looking radiant, with flushed cheeks, her black eyes shining. She belongs to this odd set of people, she is perfectly at home here, and happy. The quarrel I witnessed in the street must have been just a flare-up of temper, easily patched up, later. These people are probably engaged in some shady business, but that is no concern of mine, for I am not a police officer. I am just an interfering fool. I shall go back the way I came, drop Eveline's wallet in the letter-box of this house, and go home. A sick feeling rises in my stomach. That must be because I didn't take any real food. For it can't be that a silly mistake like this would really affect me, I ... I can't be such a fool. Quickly I turn to the window again, desperately hoping that something will happen. Anything.

I concentrate on Mochtar now. He is bringing two coffee cups to Achmad, who is still sitting on the sofa. There's something feminine about Mochtar's mincing way of walking, but it also suggests the light step of the trained boxer. He is small, but his wide shoulders aren't padded after all, I think. There was a lot of strength and experience behind that straight he placed on my jaw.

Eveline has sat down on the wooden crate, she is swaying her body to the rhythm of the radio music. It's a Latin-American melody, with a fetching little lilt. But Figel doesn't seem to like it, for he stares at the radio, sombrely. Miguel slowly sips his coffee, tapping the measure of the tune with his right foot. The two naked Greek ladies stare up dubiously at the marble burden they are carrying. A nice small international gathering. Nicely whiling away the hour.

Bert Winter saves me. I must stay a little longer, for Bert has not yet been accounted for. And I have conceived a fatherly liking for the eager student with the romantic leanings, whom Eveline left. I shall watch the play behind the glass screen a little longer. As a neutral observer, now. Completely neutral.

Eveline gets up from the crate, lifts the hem of her maroon housecoat a little, and executes a few dancing steps. I see the broad cuffs of a pair of dark-blue pyjama trousers draped over her small slippered feet. A charming picture. But neither Figel nor Miguel are interested. Figel is chewing his dead cigar, still watching the radio. Miguel lights a new cigarette from the butt of the old. A chain smoker. The two Arabs are sipping their coffee. We are neutral observers. Figel and Miguel, Achmad and Mochtar. And I.

Now Eveline turns a dial on the radio, and the music becomes suddenly very loud. Figel looks up at last. He gives her a reproachful look from his heavy-lidded eyes. But she shakes her head and points at the walls, apparently saying that they are so thick that the boarders in Pension Jansen won't be disturbed. Then she points at the French windows, and I duck, as fast as I can.

I squat there for a while, feeling cold, wet and miserable. Finally I decide to have one last look at the company before I go. When I look again I gasp involuntarily. Eveline's maroon coat and a dark-blue pyjama jacket are lying on the crate. She is standing close by the radio, in a white-satin brassière and a pair of dark-blue pyjama trousers. Her rounded shoulders and arms are very white in the glare of the unshaded lamp, her waist white and narrow between her generous bosom and her generous hips. Her resemblance to Lina makes my inside contract. Her shining eyes survey the two Arabs on the sofa, with a curiously intent, calculating look. Achmad studiously examines the content of his coffee cup, Mochtar is playing with his cigarette lighter, switching the flame on and off. Figel doesn't look at the girl either, he is contemplating the radio with raised eyebrows, as if wondering how such a small object can produce such loud music. Miguel is cleaning his fingernails with his pocket-knife. Their completely detached attitude helps me to preserve my own pose of neutral observer.

Eveline bends over and says something to Figel, still moving her hips to the rhythm of the music. Figel shrugs, then he turns round and calls out a single word to the two Egyptians. I failed to catch it, but Mochtar did. He snaps at Achmad:

"Whorehouse tricks!"

Achmad's eyes are on the girl now.

"Go get it!" he orders.

"Think I want to sleep on wet bedding?" Mochtar asks sharply.

"Do as Figel says." Achmad's voice is dull.

Mochtar says a very dirty word. He puts his coffee cup on the floor, gets up abruptly, and disappears through the door on the right.

I ought to go too. I don't know what is coming, but I know perfectly well that whatever it is, I shouldn't see it. But I stay. Eveline must be humming the words of the melody, for I see her wet lips move. Her eyes are on Figel now, almost tenderly. But Figel has got his cigar burning again, he blows puffs of smoke towards the radio. He has pushed his bowler hat so far back now that I feel it may fall off any moment. His thick hair is streaked with gray.

The door opens and Mochtar comes back. He is carrying gingerly a large bundle of white cloth. Moisture drips from it on to the floor. He walks up to Figel and asks him something, but I can't hear what he says, because of the music. Figel points with his cigar at an iron hook in the wall, by the nearest door.

Mochtar goes to the door and takes a small coil of thin cord from his right pocket. He ties one end to the corner of the wet cloth. I see it's a bedsheet of thin linen. Mochtar looks up at the iron hook sticking up out of the faded pink wall paper, then at the length of cord in his hand. He seems to hesitate.

"Cut it in two!" Achmad rasps.

Mochtar lets the smooth rope run through his fingers, with a loving gesture. His eyes stray to the window, and I quickly step aside. "It's long enough," I hear him call out.

I was just in time. The plush curtains are suddenly parted now, and a sheaf of light falls across the balcony. After a few tense moments the curtains are drawn close again.

"That'll have to do," I hear Mochtar remark. "Silly stuff!"

When I have heard him move away, I look again. While closing the curtains in the middle, he has widened the slit at the end. The right half of the room is hidden from me by a screen. The strong bulb behind it makes the wet sheet shine as brightly as a cinema screen. In its centre is the red glow of the electric heater. On the right, half hidden by the screen I can see Figel, still slumped in his chair. Miguel is gone.

The half with the sofa on my left seems very dark, by contrast. But I make out the shadowy shapes of Achmad and Mochtar, and of Miguel, who is sitting in between them now. The three men are sitting very still. I can't make out their faces.

A giant gray shadow appears on the screen, gray and blurred. Suddenly it shrinks, it becomes the black, clearly outlined silhouette of a woman, legs spread, arms raised above her head, hips swaying to the pulsating beat of the music. Eveline is dancing close to the screen, and she is stark naked.

Mochtar was right, I tell myself. This is nothing but a silly nightclub trick, a kind of strip tease. But at the same time I know that this is different. It begins where the strip tease ends. For the wet screen conceals yet reveals. It reveals all bodily details with disconcerting clarity. There is even the rose glow of the flesh as she nestles her curves close against the screen. Or is it the red glow of the heater, forming an aureole round her moving hips? Only the savage abandon saves the danced version of the act of love from becoming a shocking obscenity.

46

"You are seeing through a veil, a veil of cloth that separates you from her body. Then there is a second veil, of glass, that separates you from her world."

I have spoken aloud, and the primitive instinct of self-preservation makes me cast a quick look at the three men on the sofa. But their heads are turned to the screen, motionless. I look at Figel. He has raised his head and stares at the dancer, his heavy-jowled face as impassive as before. But he is sitting behind the screen. And he sees her in the flesh.

A sudden vertigo seizes me. The veil, the double veil is torn asunder by the upsurge of raw passion long repressed. The fire blazes up, it is the essence of all the ecstasies I ever experienced, intensified by the animal rage at the sharing of the flesh. I begin to shiver so violently that I have to steady myself by putting the palms of my hands against the window pane. Abandoning all caution I press my face against the cold glass. Every fibre of my being is identified with that beckoning shape on the screen where past and present are crudely, forcibly welded together.

At long last the music ceases, and the silhouette of the naked woman dissolves into an undefinable gray shape. And then the screen is empty again. I drop on to my knees, pressing the wet sleeve of my mackintosh to my mouth, to stifle my sobs. The sharp edges of the wooden boards cut into my knees and the cold rain falls on my bare head.

After I don't know how long I blindly grope for my hat, and scramble up. As I am standing there straightening my mackintosh, I suddenly feel very calm. I know that I have found the final solution now. My address to life has been wrong, completely wrong. Now I have found the right solution, the only solution. It blazes a clearly-defined trail, from the past to the present. And to the future.

I survey the room, dispassionately. The sheet lies in a heap on the floor. Achmad and Mochtar are still on the sofa, Mochtar relaxed, Achmad with his head bent, his elbows on his knees. Miguel is back at the electric heater, he is polishing his nails with his handkerchief. Eveline, wearing her house-coat, is standing at Miguel's side, smoking a cigarette with quick, nervous puffs. Figel reaches out with his long arm and turns off the radio which is now blaring some announcement or other. As he is about to sit back again his eye falls on the nearest Greek lady of the chimney. Pensively he stubs the burning stump of his cigar out on her rounded belly. Then he leans back into his chair, takes a large silver cigar case from his breast pocket and asks Miguel:

"Well, what about it?"

Miguel shrugs. He lets the light shine on the polished nails of his right hand. Then he says:

"Not bad."

Eveline swings round to him with an angry remark. But Figel raises his hand. He bites the tip off a new cigar, lights it and says gravely:

"Miguel is right." Perhaps he is speaking louder than before, or perhaps my senses are hyper-acute now. For I hear every word he says, very clearly. "Not bad, but not good enough for Arab spectators. They don't mind cunning capers, in bed. But when they go to see a dance, they want to see a dance." He calls over to Achmad: "Think this will do?"

Achmad raises his head. He replies slowly:

"In Beirut it might." His voice has lost its beautiful timbre, it grates. "Not in Cairo, and not in Damascus. Neither in Baghdad. They want to see the Arab belly dance."

"You see?" Figel says to Eveline.

48

"That's it, a real belly dance," Miguel tells her. "Better learn that. And get a bit fatter, old girl. They judge women by the pound over there."

Eveline ignores him.

"I could learn it, couldn't I?" she asks Figel, in German. "There must be teachers there for that kind of thing."

Figel nods ponderously.

"Don't worry," he says, also in German. "We'll cross that bridge when we come to it." German is evidently his native language.

She is smiling again. She tightens the tasselled belt of her housecoat, nods at Figel and Miguel, and goes to the door. When she has opened it, she waves her hand at Achmad and Mochtar. Then she is gone.

Miguel consults his watch.

"I'll be off too, presently. It's quarter past nine. I'll be seeing you tomorrow, on the quay."

"Don't be late," Figel warns. He looks annoyed at his cigar which has gone out again.

"My hotel is on the Zeeburgerdyk," Miguel informs him. "The phone number is doublenine-oh-six-four. Here, let me jot it down for you, together with the address. You never know."

He feels for his fountainpen. Or for a pencil. All this doesn't interest me any more. Everything has fallen into place. They are white-slavers, representing the two best markets for that merchandise, namely the Middle East and Latin America. I should have understood that at once. I go to the other end of the balcony, to the brick wall that divides it from the one of the research institute next door. I step on to the balustrade, and climb on the wall. The top is slippery and there's a sheer drop directly behind me, but I don't mind. My eyes are on the receding balcony overhead. I reach up and grab the two iron bars of the railing. As I pull myself up, my long neglected muscles ache, but I make it. I step over the railing on to the zinc platform.

The broad double window has no curtains, and there isn't a stick of furniture in the low-ceilinged room. The windows have a knob on the inside that operates a sliding rod. An easy job, I have read about it a hundred times: one presses a piece of packing paper covered with soft soap on to the glass pane, then one pushes it in. Easy. Provided you always carry a piece of thick paper and soft soap along with you, which I don't. But I discover that there's a small hole in the glass, in the lower left corner. From it two long cracks run across the pane. I wrap my handkerchief round my fingers and feel the edges of the hole. I shake the glass, with infinite care. The pane breaks with a faint tinkling sound. Now I can remove a large section. After I have propped the piece of glass up against the wall, I push my arm through the hole, turn the knob and open the window.

I quickly cross the cold room to the door. It gives on a dark landing. The only light comes from the transom over the door opposite me. The transoms of the doors on the left and the right are pitch dark. The room with the lighted transom must be hers, the attic I saw from the street below.

I knock on the door, softly.

"Who is it ?" It's her voice.

I quickly rub my face dry with my handkerchief and comb my wet hair back with my fingers. Then I push the door open.

The semi-dark attic is quite warm and the scent of a cheap perfume hangs in the air. She turns round on the iron stool, pulling the front of her housecoat close, and surveys me with raised eyebrows. I remain standing just within the open door, my wet hat in my hand. I hear the water drip on the bare floor-boards.

"You again!" she says. "Shut the door."

When I turn to her again she has got up. She points at the iron stool, and I sit down. She seats herself on the edge of the cheap iron bed. It's the only piece of furniture. Beside me is an improvised toilet table, constructed by piling three suitcases one on top of the other. On it stand a few cream boxes and small scent bottles, a water jug and a plastic beaker. A small travelling mirror is propped up against the plaster wall, flanked by two hair-brushes. The light comes from the reflector heater in the corner, burning high. I vaguely see a jumper and other articles of female apparel hanging on nails in the wall. She speaks up first.

"I can explain everything," she says eagerly. Bending her head close to me, she adds in a hurried whisper: "There's nothing wrong. The scuffle you saw in the street was just a misunderstanding, you know."

Our heads are so close that I notice the smell of her hair. Nothing separates us any more. No screen, no veil of glass.

"You are associating with crooks, Miss Vanhagen," I say evenly. "Figel probably promised to take you on a tour through the Middle East. But you'll be sold there to a brothel, and you'll never come back to Amsterdam."

"There must be some mistake, sir!" Her voice is very friendly, and persuasive. "Mr. Figel represents a number of export firms, in Lebanon. He is on his way back there now, after having made a tour of Europe, to make new contacts. The two Egyptians you saw with me are his assistants. I am frightfully sorry that you were knocked down, sir. The fact is that the two fellows had been to a bar. They began to paw me just before we went inside, and I lost my temper. It was very wrong of me to give a false name to the police, but I know that Mr. Figel doesn't like to get talked about, and it seemed the easiest solution, at the moment. You can verify everything with Mr. Figel, sir. He is downstairs." She gives me a winning smile. Her cheeks are aglow in the light of the reflector stove, her large eyes are shining. "And Mr. Figel would hardly sell me, sir! He met me in the place where I work, and when I told him that I would like to see a bit of the world, he took me on as his secretary. You were wrongly informed. Somebody in your office must have made a mistake."

This can't go on.

"It's you who are making a mistake, Miss Vanhagen," I tell her wearily. "I am not a police officer."

She shrugs impatiently.

"Of course you aren't an ordinary policeman. You belong to the special service, of the Aliens Registration Office."

"No. Hendriks is indeed my real name, and I am a bookkeeper at the Byenkorf Department Store."

"Well, if you want it that way, then ..." Suddenly she breaks off and gives me a searching look. I see that her black pupils are flecked with brown. Our eyes remain locked for a while. Then she resumes, slowly: "Yes, I believe you. But why did you come here, then?"

I take the red wallet from my pocket and give it to her.

"Because I wanted to return this to you."

She puts it on the bed beside her without giving it a second look and says:

"My address is inside. Why didn't you send it to the Oudegracht?"

I push the iron stool back so that I can lean my aching back against the wall, put my hat on the floor and take out my cigarette case. I offer her one and I light hers and mine. Then I say:

"I had noticed that you did not actually press the bell button of Pension Jansen. Since I saw a light behind the attic window of this empty house, it occurred to me that you might be staying here now, in hiding, perhaps. And the identity-card I found in your wallet proved that you had given the police a wrong name. I came here, because I thought you were in trouble and that you might need help."

She nods slowly. She draws on her cigarette and asks:

"How did you know about Figel?"

"I had to climb up here along the back of the house. Passing the balcony of the floor below just now, I paused there for a few moments and overheard part of a conversation of Figel and a man he called Miguel."

She smokes in silence for a while. Then she looks at me askance and says dryly:

"I knew one must have high qualifications in order to get a job at the Byenkorf. But I didn't know they expect their book-keepers to be expert cat burglars. I am not quite sure that you are what you claim to be, but I shall tell you the truth, regardless. You went out of your way to help me, and I wouldn't want you to think I don't appreciate that." She reaches past me and stubs out her cigarette in the cover of her cream box. Again I get a whiff of the smell of her hair, and of her body. She puts her hands into the pockets of her house-coat and resumes in a level voice: "Figel is indeed a business-man, as I told you just now, but I am not his secretary. I can't spell correctly, even! I can sing and dance, after a fashion. Not well enough to get me anywhere, ever. Figel acts as impresario, among other things. I met him a couple of months ago, in the dancing Chez Claude, where I do a singing-act. When he told me he lives in Lebanon I asked him, half as a joke, whether he couldn't arrange a tour for me, in the Middle East. He gave me his address in Beirut, and asked me to send him a picture of me, then he would see what he could do. Well, I sent him the picture, in the same spirit as one buys a lottery-ticket. But when he came back last week he told me he had fixed it, and that I could travel to Alexandria together with him, gratis for nothing."

She falls silent and gives me an expectant look. When I refrain from comment, she shrugs her shoulders and resumes:

"I shall be away for six months or so. See something of the world, and save some money, if my luck is in. The oil people there have pots of money, you know, and they are not as critical as nightclub audiences here in Amsterdam! When I am back I'll see what I'll do about my regular boy-friend here. He's a student, you know. He was rather sad when I told him I was leaving. Figel knows him too, he invited him to dinner, earlier tonight, to console him a bit, and to tell him that everything was all right."

"Everything is not all right," I say, "and my warning still stands. I have visited those parts, and I know that bars, nightclubs and whatnots there recruit their white female entertainers from Greece, Italy or Southern France, not from Amsterdam. I don't like that business with your picture either. Was it a portrait?"

"No," she says calmly, "rather more than that."

"Just as I thought. It means that Figel showed it around among some wealthy lechers there, and one said he would buy."

"I have been able to look after myself fairly well here in Amsterdam," she remarks crossly. "So I don't see why I shouldn't be able to do so in the east too."

"You don't know what you are talking about. They live by other standards, over there. Woman is still considered a chattel, and treated as such. And nobody over there will lift a finger to help you."

She bites her lower lip and knits her eyebrows. Then, all of a sudden, her mobile face lits up in a warm smile.

"You are a strange man, Mr. Hendriks, but I believe you are on the level. I shall think over your advice tonight, carefully. And your interest in me is most flattering, I must say. Why don't you take off that wet coat? While it's getting dry we could have a talk about more pleasant subjects than prospective slave-girls. About you, for instance. I'd like that very much. The people downstairs think I have gone to bed, so no one will disturb us here."

Her tone is more significant than the words. But I have the inner certainty that this is only the beginning, and I don't want it to happen in this casual manner. Therefore I get up and say :

"I'll tell you later all you want. If you decide to follow my advice, that is." I take out my wallet and scribble my phone number on one of my visiting cards. When I have given that to her, I jot down the number doublenine-six-oh-four on an old bill, for my own reference. You never know, as Miguel observed. Then I ask : "You could leave here at short notice if you wanted, couldn't you?"

"Of course. Those three suitcases contain all I have." She gets up too and asks : "If I should call you early tomorrow morning, will you come to fetch me?"

"I will. I have a Volkswagen. Ancient but still running."

Her lips brush mine. As she stands back she says, practically:

"You'd better leave by the front door. It's safer, and more comfortable, I imagine." She goes to the door and whispers: "You wait here. I'll just go down and make sure the coast is clear. There's no earthly use in creating awkward situations."

When the door has closed softly behind her, I sit down on the edge of the bed. It's a long time since I have sat thus on a woman's bed. There's a sober intimacy about it that I failed to appraise correctly when I was reconstructing the past, long ago now, before the veil was torn asunder and I discovered the present. It occurs to me that there were many other things I have been taking for granted many a year. Those will have to be re-appraised also. Formulated in other terms, at least.

She slips inside, panting a little.

"It's all right," she whispers. "I listened at the door of the large drawing-room. They are still talking busily. Good-bye!"

She gives me my hat, and presses something cold and flat in the palm of my hand.

"This is a spare latchkey. Should it turn out that you don't need it, just keep it. As a souvernir!"

She pushes me outside and the door closes noiselessly behind me.

I walk softly across the uncovered wooden floor of the landing to the narrow staircase at the end. There I pause for a moment, and listen. The house is silent. I only hear the sound of a truck that rumbles past, down below in the street. There's no stair-carpet, therefore I tread warily, so as to avoid creaking steps.

The spacious landing on the floor below is dimly but artistically lit by the street-lamp, the light of which filters inside through the stained glass of a high Gothic window. Gay patches soften the stern face of the Roman Emperor whose marble bust stands in a recess in the bare wall. Probably the marble ladies in the back room are Roman too, not Greek. Nice, cultured people lived here, people with an old-fashioned taste for Renaissance art.

I walk across the thick carpet to the head of the broad staircase. The newel is of massive oak, the sculpted top represents a life-size Janus-head with its two faces. As I lay my hand on his wooden curls a heavy weight crashes down on me.

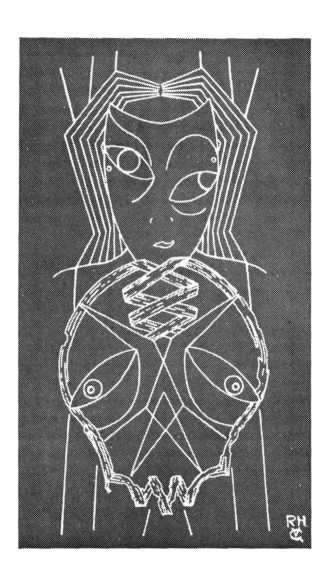

THE SNOW ON MOUNT FUJI

It is dark and cold. There's a searing pain in my lungs, and a high-pitched ringing in my ears. I want to tear the soft, clinging thing that is stifling me away from my face, but an excruciating pain shoots through my shoulders, and I know that my arms aren't there any more. The soft thing that blinds and smothers me has shifted somewhat, but now the ice-cold air cuts through my lungs as a knife. The surgeon's knife. For I am lying on the operating-table, my arms and legs are strapped to it. I want to shout, warn the nurses that the anaesthetic isn't working. But then everything becomes vague and blurred.

I wake up because of the throbbing pain that is breaking my skull apart. I gasp frantically for more air. The air doesn't cut my lungs apart any longer, it's thick and heavy, and loaded with dust. I begin to cough. The onrush of the blood will make my swollen eyes burst from their sockets, the scar on my forehead is throbbing so violently that soon it will burst too. I realize now that I have still got my arms. They are bound behind my back, and I am lying on them, on the floor, under a thick, soft blanket. I am suffocating, and I'll be dead soon. I am frozen, chilled to the bone, as befits a corpse.

I open my parched mouth wider. Now the air is red-hot, it burns my lungs. I try to swallow, and a terrible sick feeling wells up from my stomach. I retch, violently, choking on the sour fluid that fills my throat. I succeed in spitting out the fluid, but some of it has entered my nasal cavity, and I begin

59

to sneeze and cough, at the same time. Now I know what is happening. The Japs are putting me to the water-torture again. Now that I am on the verge of drowning, they'll take the wet towels away from my face. But the towels are dry, full of dust. I do get some air, but not enough, and my body dies.

I know it has died, for now I am two things: a dead body and a live mind. The body must be dead because all bodily sensations have ceased. I don't breathe, my limbs don't hurt. I am blind and deaf. But the mind is alive and alert, for a phrase is forming there. "Woman is death, and the lust for woman is the beginning of death." These words stand out clearly in my mind. I must have read them somewhere. "Woman begets death because she begets new life." It must have been a Buddhist text. There's an eternal circle that holds all beings in their self-made bondage, the bondage of their lust, their love, their hate. But I have broken through the circle because my body and all its sensations are dead. How then can all this affect me? There's a woman's name: Lina. But Lina is dead. There's also a double-faced head. What could be the connection? I can't find the answer, and I don't care. For I am mind only, and the mind is free. Free as a bird in the air. If I decide to die completely, I shall die. If I choose to remain floating in this silent world between life and death, I shall do so. Let them not take away the towels! When they take away the towels, my emotions come back and take hold of me again. First anger. Anger at Captain Uyeda, who forces on me the load of living again.

Yes, I was angry at Captain Uyeda. But I didn't hate him. Not just after the torture, when I was still two things, a dead body and a live mind. For in that first split second my mind was still high up in the cold, blue air. Moreover, Uyeda was my executioner, almost, and there's mystic bond between the killer and his victim.

We are very close, the two of us, I lying on the cement floor of the prison yard, he sitting hunched up in his iron chair, looking down at me through his large spectacles with an owlish, puzzled look. "Severe torture is an inducement to meditation, sometimes," he says in his slow, precise English. "You are angry, because I recalled you from the snow-covered summit of Mount Fuji." He straightens his spectacles and adds, pensively: "On top of Mount Wu-tai, I should say, rather. For that is what the original Chinese Zen-texts have. We say it is Mount Fuji, because Mount Fuji is our holy mountain, and because we Japanese tend to consider ourselves the centre of all things. That's a poor and unwarranted imitation of the Chinese attitude. A grave mistake for which we shall pay dearly, I fear." He sighs, and turns to the pile of flimsy sheets on the small iron desk. The notes of my interrogation.

Captain Uyeda has several sheafs of these notes before him, always. They are neatly sewn together with red string. He loves them, and I love them too. For his consulting them means a short reprieve. And I badly needed those intervals, for I was tortured particularly cruelly, Christmas 1944. Two soldiers have dragged me up from the floor and are holding me upright by my arms. One of them keeps his right hand free, always. That's the fixed routine. Captain Uyeda is still pondering over his notes. Suddenly he looks up and stares at me through his large, horn-rimmed spectacles.

"This morning you didn't say Merry Christmas to me," he says reprovingly. "It strikes me also that even in extreme pain you never call on God. You ought to, as a Christian."

"I never call upon what I don't believe in," I mumble with my bleeding lips.

Uyeda nods gravely.

"That means that you are an atheist. Tell me why."

I know that if I don't answer, the soldier on my right will hit me on the head with his stick. I'll faint, and that'll be the end of the torture. For today, at least. I have become very clever at these things. So I don't answer.

But Uyeda has given a sign to the soldier, and he doesn't strike me.

"I would really like to know," Captain Uyeda says gently. "I was ordered to attend a Christian College in Kobe for one term some years ago, to check the political views of the students and in order to improve my English. All the foreign professors there believed in God."

Unaccountably, this sober statement suddenly enrages me.

"Look at all the senseless cruelty, the brute violence, the monstrous injustice and the abject suffering in this world, all through thousands of centuries! Look at the sickening mockery we call life! How could you ever seriously believe that there's a higher power that would allow . . ."

Now the soldier on my right hits me, but not on my head. The swine hits me across my shins, hard. "Say sorry you shout at Imperial officer!" he barks at me.

I begin to cry, in frustrated rage. Captain Uyeda gives me a mildly puzzled look.

"Very interesting," he comments. "I must compare your answer with those given by our Japanese communists. I shall ask Tokyo for the records of their interrogation by the military police."

I am familiar with that puzzled look of his. When I am forced to watch the torture of other prisoners, I watch the captain instead. Then I see that same look in his eyes. He resembles a surgeon who is patiently probing the deepest secrets of the human body. This impersonal curiosity made Uyeda the worst torturer, much worse than the brutal, stupid underlings of the military police. There was the same puzzled look in his eyes when we hanged him, later. I had been chosen to put the noose round his neck as he stood there under the tree. Only his right arm had been bound behind his back, for his left had been broken when other ex-prisoners had beaten him up, with his own stick. When our doctor offered to set his arm, Captain Uyeda said: "Leave it. You'll hang me by my neck, not by my arm." All the ex-prisoners are very quiet now as they stand around the two of us, under the tree. They feel the mystic bond between the killer and his victim. When I have put the noose round his neck, Uyeda's last words are: "Please check what I used to tell you about Zen. I left my books in Japan, and I may have quoted wrongly."

When we were trying the other war-criminals, a Japanese lieutenant who had known the executed Uyeda in Japan formerly, told me that the captain had studied with an old Zen-master in Kyoto. He had made satisfactory progress, but the master had sent him away because Uyeda could not explain the final proposition put to him: "The snow melts on the summit of Mount Fuji". I can't explain that either. For the top of Mount Fuji is covered by eternal snow which never melts. I often wonder whether the proposition was perhaps quoted wrongly. For Captain Uyeda is still there, somewhere deep within me. My mind is branded for ever by his searing hot irons, by his stinging whip. I did put the noose round his neck and let him hang till death ensued. But I couldn't kill him.

The master sent him away, but nobody can sent me away. Because I am on the summit now, amidst the eternal snow, and no one can touch me. The snow is white, and the still air is blue. It's an immaculate, frozen world. The frost purifies the mind and I am now an integral part of this timeless, white world.

Suddenly I am startled by a blinding light. It's so strong that it threatens to disintegrate my mind, break up my skull in a myriad small fragments that scatter apart in a wide, empty space. The air that comes rushing into my lungs will make them burst. Uyeda, the cruel devil, is taking the towels away from my face, he is dragging me back to life again. I hear his voice, he ... No, it isn't his voice. Yet the words sound high up above me, like when he was sitting over me, hunched in his iron chair.

"He is breathing. A pity. I should have wound the blanket around his head. Tight."

Another voice enounces the sonorous Arabic formula:

"Say: Praise be to God! For you were not ordered to kill him. Not yet."

That was Achmad. Then the sullen voice of Mochtar:

"We could have called it an accident."

I see a pair of blue trousers, very close by my head. I see them through a red haze, but they are there. I see also a pair of yellowish shoes, small, and pointed. I close my puffed eyelids again. The light hurts. Every inch of my body hurts.

"He is still unconscious," Achmad says. "I hope I did not hit him too hard with my bludgeon. If he got concussion of the brain, Figel can not question him."

All the hurt feeling converges into one sharp pain in my side. Then it radiates all through my body.

"Don't!" Achmad says sharply. "If you kick his ribs in, he may yet die. He must talk first."

"He ought to die, the dirty police spy!"

"Figel is investigating, and Figel shall decide."

"The slut said she offered him to sleep with her, and he refused. That proves that he is a spy all right." There's a loud belch. "That tinned fried rice was poison, I tell you. And I can't stand this blasted damp cold. I'll light the stove."

All becomes dark again. When I come to this time, my mind is fairly clear. I am lying on a smooth floor of wooden boards. The ceiling I am looking up to is also of wood. It consists of heavy beams, slightly curved, and covered by dark-brown varnish. I close my eyes and think over what I caught of their conversation just now. It seems to be my fate to be maltreated because of silly misunderstandings. The Japanese military police mistook me for an intelligence agent, and now these people mistake me for a police spy.

With infinite care I move my head the fraction of an inch. The throbbing begins again, now at the back of my head. That's where Achmad hit me. I open my eyes. In the dark mahogany wainscoting of the wall in front of me is a copper-framed, round porthole. I know where I am now: in the saloon of a ship. But the ship is lying still, and in very quiet water, for there's no lapping of waves and she doesn't roll at all. It's the "Djibouty", the ship they were talking about. That means that we are moored alongside the Levant Quay. It's dead quiet and the porthole is dark.

The saloon seems rather large, and I am lying in a corner, carefully trussed up. A thick gray blanket is lying in a heap close by my shoulder. Craning my head further I see a door. My mackintosh and my black felt hat are hanging on a neat copper coat hanger. That's right, one should leave no clues.

And I am bound with thin, smooth ropes. A workmanlike job, neatly executed by Figel, Achmad and Mochtar, and by Eveline.

The smell of tar and fresh paint becomes mixed with the fragrance of Egyptian cigarettes. I hear the creaking of a rattan chair, then Mochtar's voice:

"Figel must find out from the wretched infidel whether he told others about Abelstraat 53. Before he came there to spy on us and to pump the slut."

"It does not matter any more. Nobody is there except the woman, and she won't talk. Figel says no one knows about this houseboat. Here we are safe."

Achmad falls silent. We are still in Amsterdam, but on a houseboat, not on the "Djibouty". The boat must be moored somewhere in a canal in a quiet part of the city, probably the harbour quarter. When Achmad speaks up again, he seems to choose his words very carefully.

"I now remember, Mochtar, that I heard you say to Figel something about a houseboat. The day before yesterday, to be precise. I did not pay much attention to it at the time. I thought I had misheard, because your English is awful. But it strikes me as curious now that you and Figel spoke about this houseboat the day before yesterday. That means before the woman had warned us about the presence of the spy, and before Figel told us he had a houseboat here that was the right place for questioning the spy."

There's a long pause. I wish they would continue, for their conversation diverts my mind from the increasing discomfort. Now that the room is warming up, the ropes begin to cut into my wrists and ankles. Suddenly Mochtar speaks up, as surly as ever.

"I can't remember in what connection Figel mentioned this boat to me."

"I assumed," Achmad says in the same careful manner as before, "that your conversations with Figel always remained confined to the practical needs of the moment. That assumption was wrong, apparently."

Mochtar does not react to that remark. After a while he says:

"I don't trust Meekhaeel. He doesn't belong to the Sheikh's men, and Figel produced him out of nothing, in Paris. The fellow asks too many questions, to my taste. Also, he said he had found absolutely nothing in the student's room. But there must be something there. Else this dirty police spy wouldn't have gone there too."

"Figel trusts Meekhaeel. If Meekhaeel says there was nothing, then there was nothing."

"What if the woman blabbed to the student?"

"The student is a young fool, he does not matter. Figel took him to a nightclub and gave him a good dinner and much strong liquor. Figel left him there, gaping at the floorshow, drunk. He should be, for the woman said he never takes alcohol." After a while he resumes: "Figel is late. It is past midnight."

That means that I have been unconscious for several hours. It all began when I put my hand on the wooden curls of the Janus head of the staircase in Abelstraat 53. Now a new day has begun, the twenty-ninth of February. The extra-day of a leap year. I have been knocked out and abducted to a houseboat, neatly trussed up, and presently I shall be interrogated, with all the trimmings. In Amsterdam, of all places. "Nothing ever happens here in Amsterdam," my friend the journalist complains often.

I can turn my head a little farther, now. Achmad is leaning back in a rattan chair. In front of him stands a low smoking table of Moorish style: a round brass platter on an ebony stand. Presumably Mochtar is sitting on the other side, but he is beyond my range of vision. On the wall hangs a coloured picture in a gilt frame. I think it is a view of Amsterdam harbour.

"Why did Figel allow the woman to bed with that wretched student?" Achmad asks. There's a trace of petulance in his voice. "He is poor and he dresses poorly. He has to use two kinds of spectacles and he does not even comb his hair. And his English is as bad as yours, Mochtar."

"Women go where their flesh sends them," Mochtar says with disdain. Only he doesn't say flesh, he uses a word from the gutter.

Achmad gives him a pained look.

"A learned old scholar once told me," he says in his measured voice, "that he had counted in our literary language forty-nine different expressions for the parts you referred to, including both direct and flowery terms. But you, Mochtar, must needs employ a foul modern word that boys will scribble on the sidewalks."

"I speak as I was taught to speak," Mochtar says sharply.

"By the prostitutes and touts who reared you."

There's a dead silence. I am expecting a violent quarrel. But Mochtar's voice is indifferent when he says:

"I have to take your insults, Achmad because the Sheikh placed you over me, just as you had to take Figel's scolding when you quarreled with that woman in the street, tonight." When Achmad doesn't react to that remark, he resumes: "Why is the Sheikh using a man of Jewish extraction, I wonder?"

Achmad sits up.

"Figel is no Jew," he says curtly.

"I don't say Figel is a Jew. I said he is of Jewish descent. I know. I smell them out, anywhere."

"You are a fool, Mochtar. Figel was a very important member of the Nazi party. The Nazis smelt out Jews better than you, and they employed Figel even for drawing up their great plan for exterminating the Jews. He succeeded in escaping from Germany when the war ended. The Sheikh got a Lebanese passport for him and helped him to get established in Beirut. For it is our duty to do what we can for the defeated Nazis who wanted to help us Egyptians to shake off the yoke of the white imperialists and the corrupt pashas who were their running dogs. The Sheikh wanted Figel to accompany us on this business trip because Figel still has many old friends all over Germany. That facilitated our buying and selling, and the collecting of the merchandise — as you have seen for yourself. And I wouldn't pass critical remarks on a man chosen by the Sheikh our master, Mochtar. The Sheikh is magnanimous, as befits a man of God. But he does not brook interference in his policies. And certainly not from you."

"Well, Figel is a clever fellow, of course," Mochtar says quickly. "And he doesn't get drunk all the time, as most of those unbelievers do. But if he drinks, he drinks plenty, and then he'll begin to talk wildly. That's what I was worrying about, you see."

Achmad takes out his gold-plated case and lights a cigarette.

"Figel never gets drunk in public," he says quietly. "And he never talks about business, not even when he is as tight as a drum. It's always about his wife, and always the same story. That they were lovers, formerly, somewhere in Poland, and . . ."

"Where's Poland?" Mochtar asks.

"Poland is a country to the east of Germany. And don't interrupt me. They were lovers, Figel said, but they got separated. He ran into her again by accident, after the war, when he was fleeing from the enemies of the Nazis, and she helped him to hide. They went to Egypt and they were married in Cairo. Thereafter he established her in a fine large house in Beirut, and he keeps no other women there, which astonishes me. For when he is drunk he will always show me her picture which he carries about with him in his wallet, and she is old and ugly, and she never begot him a child."

"You are rather talkative tonight, Achmad," Mochtar observes.

Achmad stubs out his cigarette.

"You made a stupid remark about Figel," he says evenly, "and I thought it my duty to correct you in the interest of the smooth cooperation of our team."

Achmad leans back in his chair and his face settles into a wooden expression. His eyes have that stony look orientals have when they choose to sink into a state of mental inertia, their mind a complete blank.

THE SANDALS OF THE SHEIKH

It is said in the Book of Books, the Excellent Book, that God places on no soul a burden greater than it can bear. Yet it is clearly understood that this does not absolve us from the duty to exert ourselves. And about my fulfilment of that duty I have had some doubts, these last three weeks. I should have consulted the Sheikh about my problem, before we left Cairo.

Travelling in heathen lands has not been conducive to a quiet examination of moral problems, and there is no one with whom I can discuss my difficulties. I do not count Mochtar, of course, for he is an uneducated man who is moreover most perfunctory in the observance of his religious duties. And his morose spells have become ever more frequent recently. I know the stare he gives that wretched police spy in the corner. His eyes are morose, yet there is a certain tense anticipation in them. I saw exactly the same look in his eyes before he killed the Copt, in the inner room of the Sheikh's residence. The Copt was also in a corner, but he was standing up, and he was not bound. Yet there was abject fear in his eyes when Mochtar came to stand very close to him. Mochtar said to him in his customary unpleasant voice:

"The Sheikh ordered me to tell you that he bears you no grudge."

Well I remember the look of immense, incredulous relief that came over the Copt's face. That very moment Mochtar put his hand into his right pocket and stuck his long, thin knife deep into the Copt's abdomen. Then he jerked it up with a savage jerk that cut through the Copt's entrails. The Copt sank to the floor grabbing his split stomach.

The Copt was an infidel who cheated the Sheikh, and he fully deserved to die. Yet it was an evil, unclean death. To cover up the feeling of revulsion that rose in me, I said to Mochtar, with a smile:

"Should you ever receive orders to kill me, Mochtar, do not do it in this manner!"

Mochtar shrugged. It is all the same to him. I often think that he must be mentally deficient.

When we were leaving the inner room, it occurred to me that our Sheikh, who is magnanimous, could have given the Copt at least an opportunity for saying his prayers. I would not put it beyond Mochtar to have made up the message.

"Why did you speak those words before you struck him?" I ask.

"Because the Sheikh ordered me to," Mochtar replies dully. "The Sheikh wanted the Copt to die with the peace of God in his soul."

His answer settled my foolish doubts. The Sheikh is righteous, but he is also merciful, because he is a man of God. He knows the Book by heart from beginning to end, and when he recites from it, reclining on his divan before the open window, the people in the street outside will halt in their steps and stand there, listening reverently. For despite his advanced age the Sheikh has a golden voice as he recites the Book, it vibrates with the devout submission of the true believer. We his servants are truly fortunate to be in regular attendance upon him, and to listen to his words which are the words of wisdom.

God the Great and Almighty has blessed the Sheikh with vast wealth and power, and his residence in Cairo has many halls and courtyards. Yet his private life is of austere simplicity, and his days are divided in strict accordance with the five times of prayer, as they should be.   When he has broken his fast, after the morning prayer, the Arab visitors begin to gather in the audience hall.   I see them pass my office, but I do not attend the sessions for in the morning my colleague Mohammad is on duty.   I see prominent men of our own country, trusted assistants of our President whom God shall bless because he rid us of the king and his corrupt pashas and because he crushed the Jewish hordes when they tried to invade our country.   There are also emissaries from Syria and from Saudi Arabia, and from Yemen, and from Baghdad.   The Sheikh listens patiently to each of them, and never grudges his advice. Whether it is on religious matters, or on political problems, or on questions of industry, trade and agriculture.

In the afternoon he receives foreign callers, and I am on duty.   We sit in a half circle before the Sheikh's divan, and I interpret for them, and the lower secretaries keep a record of what is being said.   For I am the Sheikh's tongue, in the languages of the infidels, as my late father Hassan al-Badawi was before me.   Mochtar is there too, because he is the Sheikh's sword.   "Try to win over your opponents with the sweet words of reason," the Sheikh once said, "but should they cling to their errors and stubbornly refuse to see the light, then crush them as you crush the flea you discover in your bedding." I bear with Mochtar because his faults are his virtues, after all. In his boyhood, in the slums, he learned to wield the knife and the strangling cord to perfection.   And after he had entered the Sheikh's service, he became a pistol expert, left-handed. For since he carries his knife and his strangling cord in his right pocket, he must keep the pistol in the left.   Knife and cord are silent, and therefore those have to be used first.

He deftly puts his hand in his right pocket now. Is he going to kill the spy before Figel has given the word? No, Mochtar knows better than that. It is his cigarette-case he takes from his pocket. I am becoming nervous, I fear. My thoughts go back to the day we left Cairo, three weeks ago now. When I had been with the Sheikh for half an hour, he summoned Figel and Mochtar. To me he said: "You shall be my tongue, Achmad, as always. Figel shall be your adviser, and Mochtar shall be your shield. Should there be new instructions, they shall reach you in the words of Figel, because I have established points of contact with Figel, all over those heathen northern lands." I am struck by a sudden thought and ask Mochtar:

"Figel did not tell you to kill the spy, by any chance?"

Mochtar gives the trussed up wretch in the corner a sour look. Then he turns to me and shakes his head. It was a stupid question. How could there have been time to communicate with Cairo? I must take hold of myself, for I am getting nervous, these days. Is it the long absence from Cairo? Or Mochtar's attitude, which has changed in a subtle manner of late? It is strange, I used to be able to read his vicious small mind as an open book.

"I must say one thing for this blasted houseboat," Mochtar remarks. "It's a good place for disposing of a dead body."

"Why?"

"Because under that small carpet over there in the corner there's a trapdoor. I had a look around, you see, while you were tying up the spy."

"You are talking nonsense, Mochtar. If you open a trapdoor in the bottom of a boat, the water will come surging inside. Even you ought to know that."

Mochtar gives me a nasty look.

"Houseboats have shallow holds," he says curtly. "After you have weighted your corpse you let it down into the hold. In the keel is a hatch which is operated from above. As simple as can be. Under the boat is four feet of water, then a thick layer of slime and mud."

"And suppose they move the boat?"

"This boat won't be moved for another year. Figel said so."

It strikes me that Mochtar knows a great deal about this houseboat. But perhaps she is not much different from our own houseboats, in Cairo.

"I am glad this boat has at least that advantage," I remark. "For in all other respects she is a mockery. Think of our houseboats, moored along the banks of the Nile the Holy! Floating homes of cultured luxury."

"You are a real, narrow-minded Cairene, Achmad. You have been away only three weeks, and already you are feeling homesick."

"A servant feels happy only in the house of his master," I remark coldly.

I am feeling uneasy, however. Perhaps I haven't been thinking so much about the Sheikh's residence as about my own quarters in its east-wing. That is another sign that I am upset, for it is unseemly to think with longing of one's wife. She was chosen for me by the Sheikh, and she suits me. She is modest, and a thrifty housekeeper. And she begot me a boy, who is handsome and clever. My nervousness is the only explanation for my sudden desire for that dancing-girl called Eveline. In Hamburg I hired a white woman but I did not sleep with her because she smelled of curdled milk. In Paris I had an Algerian woman, but I found her dull and clumsy, and her broken Arabic jarred on my ears. This woman Eveline has black hair as our women have, her eyes are black and large even without putting on kohl, and her skin is smooth and white. I had a Greek woman once, in Alexandria. She resembled Eveline, but she did not please me. Yes, now that I remember the Greek one, I know why I desired this Dutch woman. The Greek was submissive, but this girl has a fierce, independent spirit, as some Badawi women in Arabia, where my family originated. When I told her I wanted to sleep with her tonight, she slapped my face. And the spy saw it. I must give due credit to Mochtar for his presence of mind. He knocked the spy down so that we could slip inside, just before the police officers arrived. Life in these northern lands is very complicated indeed, for in Cairo no police officer would even dream of interfering with one of Sheikh Abdallah's men. It was a humiliating experience. I particularly disliked the casual way in which that woman shook hands with me afterwards, and said that the incident did not matter at all.

That woman's casual attitude was even worse than the scolding I had to take from Figel. I had to take it, because Figel was right. He is a moderate man, and wise to the ways of the world. During our complicated negotiations in Italy, France and Germany, buying and selling on the Sheikh's behalf, Figel often put in the right word at the right moment, the word that turned the scales in our favour. I did not like, however, his ready acceptance of Meekhaeel's offer to join us, when we were in Paris. Could it be that Figel, after all that we Arabs have done for him, still prefers the company of a white man of his own creed?

The grating voice of Mochtar cuts into my musings. Fidgeting in his chair he says:

"The trouble is that the corpse must be weighted. And I don't see anything to weight it with."

"This boat should have an extra anchor-chain," I say impatiently. "Use that!"

"Yes," Mochtar says pensively, "such a chain might do. It might do very well, in fact."

The premature worries of this vulgar little man having thus been disposed of, I can turn my thoughts to Cairo again. I think of that last day, before we left for the airfield. Early in the afternoon I was sorting out old letter-files, in the vaulted room, next door to my office. At the back of a pile of dusty expired contracts dating from the time my late father was the Sheikh's confidential secretary, I found a document, written in the Sheikh's own impeccable running hand. It spoke of wholly unbelievable, of monstrous things. It confirmed that he, the Sheikh, had sold through a Lebanese middleman large tracts of land in Palestine to the accursed Jews, thereby contributing to the establishment of their so-called state, on territory stolen from our Arab brethren.

Utterly confused I rushed upstairs, to the hall where the boy Ismael was preparing coffee for the visitors who were to arrive soon. With trembling hands I gave the document to the Sheikh. After one glance at it he said quietly to Ismael: "You may retire, my child. Tell all those who come to wait in the anteroom, for a brief while." And to me: "Pour me a cup, Achmad, for in my advanced age the brain gets dull, and it needs the fragrant stimulant."

When he had taken his coffee he gave me a sad smile and said, calling me affectionately by my father's name: "Son of Hassan, for you I have no secrets, and you shall now hear of things no one has heard before. When the Jews embarked upon their sordid scheme in Palestine, the Arab brethren were in confusion, and the white imperialists utilized our confusion for harming and humiliating us Arabs, as is their wont.

Messengers came to me from Jeruzalem the Holy, and from Beirut, and from Damascus, and what they told me roused a great anger in me, and I wanted to crush the evil Jewish plan in the bud so as to prevent the Jewry of the world from gathering in one place. But then God in His infinite Mercy granted me an illumination, in the line: 'Thy Lord shall gather thine enemies in one place so that thou canst destroy them all and forever.'" The Sheikh heaved a deep sigh and resumed: "I shall not speak to you of the future, son of Hassan, because the future is in God's hand, and He knows best." But then he recited the chapter that is called that of the Elephant, saying: "Seest thou not in what manner thy Lord dealt with the companions of the Elephant? Did He not crush their treacherous scheme?" After having thus cited the Book, he folded the document and gave it to me saying: "This paper was retained by an unfortunate oversight which you shall now set right." And he pointed at the silver brazier which the boy Ismael uses for preparing the Sheikh's water-pipe.

I placed the document on the glowing coals, and as the smoke curled up and dissolved in the air, so all my misplaced doubts dissolved. I bowed low to thank my master for passing over a grave mistake made by my late father. Then my eye fell on his leather sandals which were lying on the floor before his sofa. To show him my humble gratitude I said: "Allow your servant to offer you, saving your presence, a pair of new sandals. For these are old and worn and they might hurt your feet." But the Sheikh raised his hand and spoke: "You shall not do so, Achmad, for these sandals though old are still serviceable. Thrift becomes a true believer, and I never discard what is still of service to me. Should the day come when it is of no use any longer, then only do I discard it — not without a pang of regret inspired by the parting from what served me loyally for many years."

He took another sip of his coffee, then asked suddenly: "How many are there in my humble house who serve me, Achmad?" I counted them over in my mind and replied: "About seventy men, may God lengthen your days." He nodded gravely and said: "All those are loyal men, Achmad. But there is only one among them whom I trust as I trust myself. It is therefore that I appointed you to fill the place vacated by the late Hassan al-Badawi your father, the peace of God be on his soul."

These words moved me deeply. I wanted to speak, but the Sheikh raised his hand again and pursued: "It is therefore, son of Hassan, that I shall entrust you with an important mission that is both delicate and dangerous. You shall travel to the northern countries, and there conduct on my behalf certain transactions to which I shall return anon. Now I only want to warn you that these transactions must be kept secret. If the authorities of the countries concerned would come to know about them, they would use this knowledge to harm and humiliate us Arabs, as is their wont. Also, there are certain persons there who oppose me and who might try to make the mission fail. Now you are an expert in foreign languages but you have not had any practical experience of the laws and of the customs in those benighted heathen lands. Therefore I have decided to assign to you an able assistant, and an able bodyguard." The Sheikh clapped his hands, and when the boy Ismael appeared, he ordered him to summon Figel and Mochtar. The three of us left that same night for Rome, by aeroplane.

And now, after three weeks, we have successfully completed the mission, and tomorrow we shall go back to our own country again, on the ship "Djibouty". I am in a nostalgic mood and I say to Mochtar:

"I wish we were back in Cairo already, Mochtar."

Mochtar has been staring at the prisoner again. Now he turns his head to me, and he says in his dull voice:

"You shan't go to Cairo, Achmad."

Now I must say something, anything to prove to Mochtar my aloof attitude. But I can not find the right words, I need time, time to think. Yet at that very moment I know that I do not need time to think. For the knowledge that I would not see Cairo again had been at the back of my mind, all the time. I knew it, but I did not want to know it. However, my petty regret is at once replaced by a warm glow of great satisfaction. This important mission was entrusted to me as a sure token of recognition. The forbidden knowledge I obtained from the document my father failed to destroy necessitated of course my elimination. But instead of having me removed at once, the Sheikh granted me a reprieve, so as to give me an opportunity to make amends for my late father's oversight by carrying out the present difficult mission. Since the mission was a success, the father's mistake and the son's merit have now cancelled each other out. Nothing will mar the Sheikh's memories of the al-Badawis, father and son. He will agree that we served him to the best of our limited abilities, that we served him as faithfully as his sandals. And the fact that the Sheikh granted me this last favour proves that he thinks the sandals have worn well. A servant needs to know only whether his service has been satisfactory. His master's affairs do not concern him. It does not behove me to reflect upon the Sheikh's transaction with the Jews. All judgement rests with God the Merciful, for He knows better.

I rise and pronounce the required formula:

"Verily to God we belong, and verily to Him we return."

I cross my arms and look down at Mochtar. But he, the miserable guttersnipe, he can not bring up the dignified attitude that befits this solemn moment. He fidgets in his unpleasant manner and he avoids my eyes. I ask:

"The pistol?"

Mochtar nods.

"And here and now?"

He nods again, his eyes downcast. The thought of the cold slime and mud under this boat chills me. I see the warm blue waves of the Mediterranean. I would have preferred it to happen on the ship, with the coast of my dear country within sight. But it can't be helped, it was written that it would happen here. 1 am about to tell Mochtar to hurry and get it over with, but then he looks up at me.

"I have been dreading this moment," he mutters crossly, "all these three weeks." To my astonishment I see a shy look in his large eyes. "Why couldn't we have been friends, Achmad? We lived in the same house and we served the same master. I have always been rather unpleasant to you, Achmad. But I had to. Because I always envied you. And because I didn't want you to know that I have a sneaking admiration for you, for your virile strength. You make me think of long rides through the desert, with a friend, in the cool of night under the starry sky, when ..."

"You have been reading your paltry dime-novels again, Mochtar!" I say with disgust. "What would you know about the desert, you who were raised in the slums of Port Said?"

"Yes, that's where I was raised, Achmad. But I had a friend there once, a tall sailor from Oman. We used to sit on the quay, at night. And he would tell me many stories about his life in the desert, formerly. He may have lied a lot, but they were damned good stories, anyway. About Arab knights riding through the desert, brandishing their swords, like you see in the movies. That tall sailor had your long stride, Achmad, and your powerful thighs. The horseman's thighs."

I see he is in dead earnest, and I decide to tell him.

"I shall explain why we could never be friends, Mochtar. I shall explain it by telling you about something that happened, one night, about a year ago. You will remember that the summer was very hot that year. Even in the roofgarden of the Sheikh's residence the air was hot and close, and tepid water came from the fountains in the front courtyard. I left by the main gate for a walk along the quay of the Nile. Then a young woman who had been squatting at the foot of the wall rose and approached me. She was dressed as a prostitute, there were silver bangles on her wrists and ankles, and she was small and slender, like a boy. She did not say a word, but her eyes were very large and brilliant above the veil that covered the lower part of her face. She was beautiful, Mochtar, and I was thinking of going with her."

Mochtar rises.

"And why didn't you?" he asks, his face taut.

"Because all of a sudden I remembered what was behind all those outer charms. Nothing but a vulgar, scheming mind."

Mochtar nods slowly.

"Yes, you were probably right, Achmad. I was very angry with you that night, but I am not angry with you now. For you said you thought she was beautiful. That gives me something sweet to think about, when I am feeling low. You don't know how low I feel sometimes, Achmad. You are an educated man, you can think of so many pleasant things when you are feeling low. But I just feel rotten. And never as rotten as now."

He comes up to me, and his hand moves to his left pocket. A sudden thought strikes me.

"What has been decided about my wife?" I ask.

"I said she's beautiful, didn't I?" Mochtar snarls. "She's the Sheikh's property, just as your son. Good merchandise."

I stare into his flashing eyes, stunned. He moves his hand to his right pocket and I feel a blow in my stomach so hard that it makes me stagger back. And he said ... he said it wouldn't be the ...

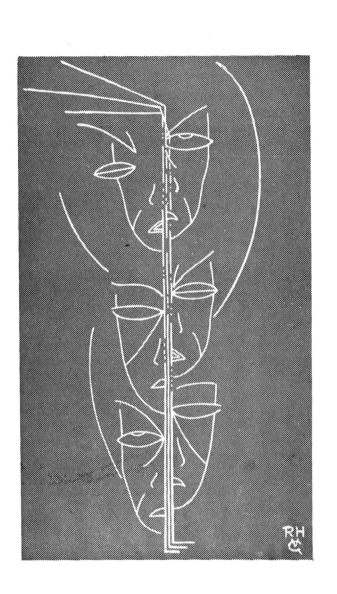

FIREWORK ON THE CANAL

Seeing him being ripped apart makes my stomach heave. I raise my head from the floor in a frantic effort to get rid of the sour vomit that is almost choking me. Tears blind my eyes.

A hard kick against my shoulder makes my head hit against the floor again. Half opening my stinging eyes, I see Mochtar's distorted face directly above me. Saliva drips from his working mouth, he seems to be crying and laughing at the same time.

"I kill you, you dirty swine! I . . . " He chokes on the words.

His foot shoots out again, missing my head by the fraction of an inch. I manage to roll over, in a desperate attempt to get away from his pointed brown shoes. I land with my head against the wall with a thud that half stuns me.

"What are you doing? Stop that, Mochtar!"

It's Figel's voice. Then there's a loud explosion. And a second one.

The silence that follows is so deep that I begin to wonder dazedly whether the two blasts, very loud in the closed saloon, have made me deaf. I am lying completely still, my face pressed against the smooth wood of the wainscoting.

After I don't know how long, I hear someone mutter. Then I catch a few words:

"One hell of a mess!" It is Miguel.

I want to call out to him but I can manage only an ineffectual spluttering noise. Apparently Miguel has noticed me. I hear his light steps, then a large brown shoe turns me over on my other side.

"You are still alive, eh?" Miguel remarks sourly.

I have another attack of nausea.

"Make me sit up!" I gasp.

He drags me by my collar across the floor towards Achmad's chair and lets me down in it, rather carelessly. All my bones and muscles ache, and the ropes bite into my wrists and ankles. Even so it's an immense relief to be in an upright position again, at last.

Miguel stands himself in front of me. His heavy overcoat is hanging open and shows his admirable tweed-suit, as immaculate as before. But his face is chalk-white and small beads of perspiration pearl on his forehead. He feels in his waistcoat pocket and takes out a small, flat aluminium box. With a shaking hand he puts a green pill between his lips. Then he looks me up and down, and a slow grin spreads over his face.

"God, you do look an awful mess!" he says cheerfully.

He pulls the handkerchief from my breast-pocket, wipes my cheeks and my chin, then he throws it on the floor. "You are a mess," he repeats. "But not as bad as your three friends!"

He stands aside. I quickly avert my eyes from Achmad who is lying on the floor in a pool of blood. Mochtar looks peaceful, at first sight. He is sitting on the floor, his back against the wall, his legs stretched out in front of him. His blue trousers are still neatly creased, but his head is sagging over his right shoulder and a thin stream of blood is trickling slowly from the hole under his left eye. A small pistol is lying by his left hand. Figel is nowhere to be seen.

"Where is Figel?" I ask.

Miguel silently points to my left.

As I turn my head I see Figel. He is sprawling on the floor, one leg stretched out, the other drawn up against his large stomach. His arms are flung out, as if he had been trying to break his fall in the approved judo-manner. His right hand is grasping a heavy automatic. His large, sallow face is peaceful, but his throat and breast are a mass of blood.

Miguel lights an Egyptian cigarette. I gratefully inhale its fragrance. For now that Miguel has cleaned my face and I don't notice my own stench so much, the raw smell of the blood and cordite makes me feel ill again. Miguel points at Figel and says in a bitter voice:

"The fat bastard promised to get me safely to Egypt! And he gets himself shot dead by a damned nigger! Let's see whether he can at least help me to a bit of pocket money."

He kneels by the corpse and with thumb and forefinger opens Figel's coat.

"Couldn't you cut my ties first?" I ask, as an experiment.

He looks up at me, over his shoulder.

"Be glad that you're still alive, old boy," he remarks coldly.

I look on as he expertly searches the dead man's pockets. The small change and a key ring he puts back, but the bulging wallet stuffed with papers and green American banknotes he transfers to his own pocket. He opens the large silver cigar-case and sniffs at the long cigars. "Expensive brand!" he mutters. "Those will help to console me." Stuffing the cigar-case in his side pocket, he gets on to his feet again and starts to search the two dead Arabs. I close my eyes for I can't stand that messy sight. When the creaking of rattan tells me that he has sat down in Achmad's chair, I look again. Miguel is absorbed in a small black notebook.

"What happened?" I ask. I hardly recognize my own voice.

Miguel looks up. He puts the notebook in his pocket and lights a new cigarette. He studies me for a while before he replies:

"What happened? Well, you saw that for yourself, didn't you? I drove Figel here, and he was out of the car like a flash. I stayed behind the wheel, to park that old car nicely. When I came inside, it was all over. Figel must have come in just after the small fellow had cut his friend's guts. Figel doesn't approve of that and he draws his automatic. But that small devil, that's a trained killer, I tell you. He must have had that toy-pistol of his near at hand, and he shoots Figel through his throat. Neat. Now you tell me who shot first, Figel or the Gypsy? The shots sounded awful close, to me."

"I couldn't tell you. I only saw how the small man murdered the other. Then he began to kick me, and I rolled over, with my face to the wall, as you found me just now. I heard Figel shout at the small fellow to stop kicking me, then the two shots. You might check those two pistols."

"Still trying to play the smart little cop, eh? Tell your story! Everything!"

"I want a cup of coffee first."

"And hot rolls, and fried eggs, sunny side up!" He gets up and slaps my face. "Talk, bastard!"

The slap makes my head reel, but it doesn't affect the cold clarity that is in the back of my mind. And I have felt under my feet something hard and flat on the floor. That's promising, for Mochtar's knife is nowhere in sight. It all depends on what Miguel is going to do. I tell him my story, the relevant facts; beginning by my witnessing the assault on Eveline and ending up with a brief account of our conversation up in her room. I give him to understand that I watched him and Figel from the balcony a couple of minutes only, before climbing up to Eveline's floor.

When I am through, Miguel sadly shakes his head.

"You are even a bigger fool than I thought you were," he says glumly. "So you got yourself into this mess not because you have to earn the city's salary, as I thought at first, nor in order to blackmail us or to cut yourself in, as I thought later, after I had heard Eveline's story. You just did it because you got a yen for that silly dame who imagines she's dancing when she shakes her tail. Can't sing either, for that matter. I know you are not a cop and not a crook, for Figel did some checking, after the two Gypsies had taken you here. You are a book-keeper in a department store. Holy Heaven, how stupid can a man get?"

"What's going to happen to the girl now?"

"Happen? Nothing, of course. She'll have to shift for herself. I am not a white-slaver, thank you. Too much risk and too little profit."

"And what are you going to do about me?"

He looks me over with undisguised distaste.

"You? Throw you overboard. You stink."

"What about a cup of coffee first?"

"All right. I could do with a cup myself."

As he is turning round I ask:

"What about cutting my ties?"

He says a rude word and disappears through a small door. It is in the opposite corner, I hadn't noticed it before. I close my eyes, for the strong light of the ceiling-lamp is still hurting them.

Miguel comes back with two cups. One he puts on the table, the other he brings to my lips. I drink greedily. He has made it white, fortunately. Then he sits down, stretches out his long legs, and slowly sips his own coffee, which is hot and black. I must admit that Miguel is considerate, after a fashion. When he has finished the coffee he lights a new cigarette and says:

"I have decided what I shall do with you, old boy. Stupid, clumsy bastard as you are, you can still make yourself useful to me. I am not a white slaver, and I am not a killer and I don't want to be put on record as such. You shall be my star-witness." He looks at his wrist-watch. "It's now one o'clock. In three maybe four hours, before I blow, I'll phone the police. Tip them off that they can find three dead bodies on this houseboat, and one trussed-up fellow who'll be glad to explain what it's all about. In due time they'll come here, and then you tell them the truth. Always a good policy to tell the truth, old boy. To the police, that is."

"And what is the truth?" I ask.

He gives me a suspicious look.

"The girl told us you had caught on all right. They were collecting women for the Middle East, of course. Got most in Italy and France, and some very good stuff in Hamburg. They were going to pick them up in Marseilles. Or in Genua, maybe."

"But Eveline is here."

He shrugs his shoulders.

"She was a special order, I gathered. To be delivered in Beirut. Figel was rather cagey, about her. He took her boy friend out tonight, so that I could go over his room. To check whether she hadn't left anything behind there that proved she was leaving with Figel. You fooled me neatly, then, I grant you that!" He grins ruefully, and adds: "If you have still got that yen for her you'd better tell her to stick to Amsterdam!"

"You say you aren't a white-slaver. Where do you come in, then?"

He gets up, lights a cigarette and puts it between my lips.

"Well," he says judiciously, "that part of your story you'll have to edit a bit, old boy, if you know what I mean. I ran into Figel in Paris a fortnight ago, when I happened to be a bit hard pressed, by the French cops, you know. An over-confident elderly lady suddenly grew over-suspicious, she ran to the police and told them nasty things about me, involving a piece of jewelry, if I understood it correctly. Figel got me out, I must say for the fellow that he had good connections. He said he'd take me to Egypt, where the French can't touch me, and get me a brand-new passport. My job was to act for him and the two Gypsies as a decoy. Easy job, for the girls have a way of falling for me. An easy job, but not a nice job, to me. If your profession is to bed down with mature ladies, you come to hate it. Like poison."

I know why Mochtar killed Achmad, for I got the trend of their last conversation. But I am interested in what Miguel has to say about them. So I ask:

"Why did the small man murder his colleague?"

Miguel shrugs.

"They didn't get along. The young one thought he could use the other's share in the profit, so he killed him. Figel told me that the tall one was the boss, but I have eyes in my head, and I knew that the fellow had been earmarked as the scape-goat. Figel and Mochtar — that's the name of the small killer — let the other do all the risky jobs, always." He sighs. "Now there'll be a nice crowd of carefully selected cuties waiting in vain in Marseilles. Or in Genua, perhaps."

"Pity you don't know where exactly," I remark. I spit out the cigarette that is singing my moustache.

"Don't get nasty now, old boy! I am not dealing in that kind of merchandise, I tell you. My business is with dames of a certain vintage, wealthy and lonely, preferably tourists. I am a travel guide, you see, privately conducted tours, very privately! I work within the limits of the law, mostly. I can't refuse presents, can I? That would be impolite. Now you'll understand why I don't want my name listed with Interpol, and certainly not as a suspected white-slaver. It would ruin my business. So here is what you tell the police about me. I am a man of the world, and Figel asked me to take him to a few selected bars and nightclubs and so on. But I found out that he was a white-slaver, and when I came across you spying on them, I passed on everything I knew to you. You add that I am a kind of confidence man, and hence a bit shy. So instead of reporting to the police personally, I cleared out."

"And why should I do that for you?"

He gives me an appraising look, cocking his fair, curly head.

"Because you are straight, as far as I can see. And because one good turn deserves another. I am not a killer. But if I didn't phone the police and left it to chance whether you were discovered in time on this houseboat on this lonely stretch of the canal, that wouldn't make me a killer, would it now?"

I shiver involuntarily. Yet my curiosity prompts me to ask one more question.

"I would hardly like that, of course. But wouldn't it be simpler for you? Walk out of here and forget all about me, I mean?"

"You are so goddamned stupid that I wonder how you managed to stay alive in this bad bad world! I have been seen about with Figel and the two Gypsies, stupid, in plenty of places, and public places too. After the police have found the mess here on this boat, they'll set to work. Show pictures around, ask questions, and so forth. They'll be on to me in no time. Never underestimate the police, my friend, they are competent professionals."

"And after they have heard my story, they won't look for you too energetically. Yes, I see your point now. All right. If you give me another cup of coffee, it's a deal."

He goes to the narrow door again. Evidently there's a kitchen of sorts, or a pantry.

After he has made me drink, he sits down. He doesn't seem to be in any hurry. Perhaps he is waiting for something. Or for someone. Or has the business here so upset him that he needs my company, for a while? The green pill he took looked like a sedative to me.

"The police will want to know more details," I say. "Whether Figel and his men were on their own, for instance."

He raises his left eyebrow and considers this for a while.

"No," he says, "I think the big boss is a party in Cairo. Nasty chap, from what I heard. Dabbles in politics, company promoting, arms traffic, and traffic in anything with money in it. A gangster-boss. But in Middle East-style, of course."

"Were the girls destined for Cairo, then?"

"That I don't know. Perhaps the boss wanted to sell them to an expensive bordello. Or he meant to forward them gratis to his Arab business relations, with the season's greetings. You may embroider that as much as you like, for that is one fellow the police will never get to. Those guys pull a lot of strings, you know. Just like in the States."

"You speak with an American accent. Are you a naturalized American citizen?"

"Mind your own business, will you?" he says curtly. He draws on his cigarette, then he goes on in a more friendly tone: "My father was a Dutch naval officer, my mother an Argentine dancer. My father died in the war, my mother married a cad, in Buenos Aires, and I joined a circus. Did a damned fine turn there, after a few years. Trapeze, tightrope, the high jump — you should've seen me, in my pink tights, all covered with gold! I liked it, and the public liked it. Good God, you should've seen the women that tried to suck up to me, after the show. And real ladies, mind you! Well, then my heart let me down, and the doctors told me to chuck my job. So I limited myself to parlour athletics. There's good money in that too. Next year I'll have saved up enough for buying myself a bungalow on the beach, and a small boat. In Naples, or in Beirut. Do some fishing, and all by myself, mind you! To hell with all women! I wouldn't be seen dead with those bitches I have to bed with. But with that rotten ticker of mine that's exactly what might happen to me, some day!"

He laughs at his own joke, rather bleakly. He rises, buttons his overcoat, and says:

"Good-bye, old boy! Pray that nothing happens to me. Not before I have made that call to the police, at least!"

I wait till I have heard him start the car and drive off. Then I scrape and push with my numbed feet. It was indeed Mochtar's knife that had landed under my chair. That Miguel overlooked that is another proof of his being very upset. I wonder what really happened while I was lying with my face to the wall. Then I set to work. I am prepared for a long and arduous job, but it might have been worse. The most difficult part proves to be to let myself down from the chair on to the floor. Thereafter some wriggling about gets my bound hands over the knife fairly soon, and after I have got it in the right position, the rest is easy. I get some nasty cuts in my fingers, though, for it is hairsharp. When my hands are free I suck my wounded fingers and massage my bruised wrists for a while. Then I cut the ropes round my ankles.

Sitting on the floor with my back to the dead men I inspect my pockets. Everything is there, even the tin tube with the precious tablets, and the money in my wallet. Getting to my feet is agony, but I make the door, and get my cigarettes out of the pocket of my mackintosh. I need one badly, for I have soiled and wetted myself, and that with the stench of the blood makes the air almost unbearably foul. I turn the electric stove off and stumble to the narrow door.

There's a small but well-equipped kitchen, with a gas water-heater over the sink. After I have cleaned my suit as well as I can, and washed myself thoroughly with hot water, I begin to feel better. I find a bottle of beer and a chunk of cheese in the larder, and after that I feel better still. Finally I make myself a cup of coffee. I take it black and strong, this time.

It is dead quiet outside. I am feeling too weak yet for going out to see where I am exactly. So I remain sitting there, in the kitchen chair, my arms resting on my knees. I try to assess the situation. I reflect that Captain Uyeda should not have carped about the Jap Zen-masters substituting the summit of Mount Fuji for that of the Chinese Mount Wu-tai. I haven't the slightest idea of what Mount Wu-tai looks like, but I know Mount Fuji from innumerable pictures and coloured postcards. Its top, clad in eternal snow, pure and white against the azure sky, has always seemed very beautiful and impressive to me. Since now the contact with time and place has been re-established, I am no longer there on that snowy, time-less summit. But that doesn't matter any longer, for I have been actually there, and the still blue air and the frozen whiteness are still with me, deep within me; I shall possess them forever, whether alive or dead. Captain Uyeda was a bungler, after all. He did not bring me close enough to death. He only let me ascend Mount Fuji's slope, so that I could get a fleeting glimpse of its frozen summit.

I feel vastly superior to Uyeda now. I am convinced that if I would ponder long enough on the final proposition that baffled him, I shall find the right answer. "The snow melts on the summit of Mount Fuji." I think it over for a while but that doesn't get me anywhere and the strenuous thinking only makes me sleepy. Anyway, Eveline, Achmad and Mochtar did much more for me than Captain Uyeda, between the three of them. Eveline set ablaze the fire that cauterized the past, Achmad neutralized the present by hitting me on my head, and Mochtar brought me in the required proximity to death by trying to suffocate me with the blanket. And now I am free.

All the questions I have been brooding over these last years are not there any more. They were non-existent to begin with, for we human beings are not responsible to each other. We can not really give each other anything, not even love. And we can not really take anything from each other, not even life. Each follows his own particular course through a timeless and limitless void. All the rest is illusion, a figment of our poor, deluded minds.

If I remain sitting here much longer, I shall fall asleep. I get up and open the kitchen door. It gives on a narrow platform, on the stern of the houseboat. By the helm are stacked three gasoline drums and two large dust-bins. A gangway leads up to the cobbled quay. It has stopped raining, but the stones are still shining wet. The houseboat is moored in a long, broad canal. Further along stand a few dark houses, then there's a long, high wall, presumably of a godown. A lonely crane is silhouetted against the night sky. It is very quiet, the noise of the city doesn't penetrate here. Figel has chosen the location well. I have never been in this section of the harbour quarter before, but I know it can't be far from the Zeeburgerdyk Miguel mentioned to Figel.

The cold, crisp air makes me shiver, so I pull the door shut and go back to the saloon. I cross it without looking at the three dead bodies, and quickly open the door where they had hung my coat and hat. It gives on a small lobby. Apart from the main entrance there's also an oak-panelled door on the left. This one leads into a bedroom, not too large but well furnished. More than half of the space available is taken up by an enormous double bed, covered with an embroidered eiderdown. There's a luxurious toilet-table with a large round mirror over it, a double wash-basin, and a white-lacquered wardrobe. On the wall hangs a coloured picture in a heavy gilt frame. It represents a buxom naked woman with long fair hair, squirming in the iron-clad arms of a Lohengrin-like knight. Sentimental and cruel — love in the Teutonic manner. The wardrobe is empty, and so is the small cupboard. The room is damp and cold, but the expensive electric heater in the corner shows that it can be nice and warm, if so desired.

I light a cigarette and go back to the saloon. I quickly pick up the blanket and put it over Achmad's legs and abdomen. Then I contemplate the three bodies — of men who dealt in living bodies, which in turn become dead bodies, some sooner, some later. The abomination of the flesh. And Miguel is right, of course. These crimes can never be brought home to the real perpetrator, that pure old party in Cairo. I nearly get sick again so I go quickly to the kitchen.

There's a pile of dish-towels on the shelf over the sink. I make a small cut in the seam of one with my penknife, and find that I can easily tear the cloth into long, thin strips. These I tie together, till I have got two lines, each of about ten meters long. That should do. There's a bottle of salad-oil in the larder, and I pour it into a pewter pan. I neatly roll up one line and put it in the pan. Then I go to fetch the three gasoline drums. One I place beside Achmad, and another between Figel and Mochtar. I open the third drum, and pour half of its content over the dead men. Then I go back to the kitchen, take the line from the pan and squeeze it dry. As I am twisting it together with the dry one, I reflect that this ought to make a good, slow-burning fuse. One end I push under the kitchen door, then I walk to the saloon, laying out the line in an artistic zigzag pattern. The end I tie to a button of Figel's coat. I wet my fingertip and hold it close to the floor. There's a slight draught. Enough for fanning the fuse, not enough for blowing it out. I put on my hat, switch off the lights, and leave by the kitchen door. Before closing it behind me, I light the end of the fuse with my cigarette-lighter. It burns well. I estimate I have got from twenty minutes to half an hour.

A hurried walk along the deserted quay brings me to the dark row of houses. I turn a corner at random, then another. I halt in front of the steam-covered window of a bar. Next door is a grocery shop, all dark, but a light is burning behind the pink curtains of the second floor. When I have pushed the bell button, the latch is pulled back after a remarkably short interval. That means that this is the right address. I slip inside and crane my head at the blowsy young woman who is standing at the head of the steep staircase, the cord that operates the latch still in her hand. Her dressinggown hangs open, showing her short pants of black lace and her black brassière. I take a silver coin of two-and-a-half guilder from my pocket and throw it up.

"I need a taxi, double quick," I say. "This will help to pay your telephone bill."

She picks up the coin and calls down:

"Add eight of the same and you can have yourself a cosy rest. Breakfast included."

"Many thanks, but I just had everything I needed. I'll be in next time."

She shrugs and says:

"Pull the door close when you leave, will you. It sticks a bit."

Standing in the small, dimly lit lobby that smells of cooked cabbage, I look steadily at my wrist-watch. In exactly seven minutes the cab is there. I know. These places have their own arrangements. And nobody talks.

"Everything to your satisfaction, sir?" the chauffeur asks as we drive off.

"Excellent," I say.

"Yes, I never had complaints about Truus. Coughs up only two guilders for me, though, when I take a chap to her address. Ought to be five, that's the regular commission. But she's a good girl, never makes trouble. That means a lot, in my line of business."

When we are passing through the avenue off Abelstraat, I tell him to stop. I pay him the fare and an extra-tip, not too large, not too small. I must be one of many. I wait till the cab has disappeared round the corner, then I saunter on, my hands in my pockets.

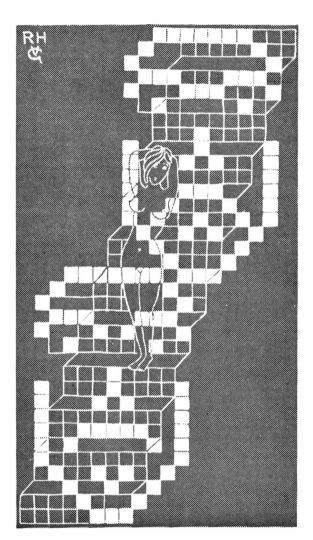

JANUS ON THE STAIRS

The streetlamps cast their bleak light on the long, empty stretch of the curb. From across the street I look up at the top floor of No. 53 and I see that there's still a light behind the attic window. Crossing over to the house, I notice that the rain is coming down again, in large, ice-cold drops. I open the frontdoor with the latch-key she gave me. That had been a clever move, for it put me completely off my guard. And she thought she wouldn't be needing the key any more, anyway. I slowly climb the broad, carpeted staircase.

I halt when I have arrived on the first landing, for the climb made me realize that I am dog-tired. Standing there at the head of the broad staircase, I place my hand on the sculpted Janus-head that tops the massive newel. As I did before. Five hours before, or five minutes. Janus is the god of all going out and coming in, he doesn't mind the time. Am I going out or coming in? I am also facing two ways, and I don't quite know what to do about it. All right, let's say that it was five minutes ago when I said good-bye to her, in her small, cosy room on the next floor. Let's say I repented when I was halfway down these stairs, and decided to go back up to her room. As I am doing now.

The transom above her door is lit by the same faint red glow as before. I stand still for a moment and listen. Someone is moaning inside. I knock and say loudly:

"It's me, Hendriks."

The moans stop. There's the creaking of bedsprings. Soft steps of slippered feet, then the door opens. I remain standing there, stockstill, in blank astonishment.

She is clad in Eveline's blue pyjama suit, but she can't be Eveline. This puffed, feverish face, these lacklustre eyes, heavily ringed! A black lock sticks to her moist forehead, the pyjama jacket hangs sloppily down from her hunched shoulders.

"Come inside," she says in a grating voice. "There's a draught."

She shivers, although the room is warm. She takes her housecoat down from the nail in the wall, throws it over her shoulders, then she sits down on the edge of the bed, her arms folded inside the coat, pressed close to her breast. I put my hat on the floor and sit down on the iron stool, by her improvised toilet table of the three suitcases.

"The pain is terrible," she gasps. "And Figel is dead. God, I need him!   And he is dead."

I stare at her haggard face. Miguel must have been here before me, and he has told her. Unbelievable as it seems, she must have been in love with Figel. She bends over, her head close to mine. But she doesn't see me. Pressing her hands against her stomach she begins to moan again, swaying her body to and fro. I must try to divert her attention.

"Did Miguel tell you that the two Egyptians are dead too?" She nods.

"It doesn't matter," she whispers. "They didn't know Figel had his own supply. God, what shall I do?"

She shivers so violently that her teeth begin to chatter.

Suddenly I understand. Her radiant beauty earlier in the night, her brilliant eyes, her flushed cheeks, her exuberant abandon in flaunting her naked charms. And the consummate skill in acting she displayed when I came to see her, and the clever way she formulated her vague stories. I failed to understand, I, an expert! But I can help her, by a fortunate chance. I unbutton my mackintosh, take the tin tube out and give her one tablet.

"Take it, it will relieve the pain."

I pour water from the jug in the plastic beaker. She asks no questions, she swallows the tablet, meekly as a child.

"When Miguel came," she says dully, "it wasn't hurting so badly yet."

"What did Miguel come here for?" I ask.

"To look for Figel's money, of course. I went downstairs because I heard someone move about in Figel's room, down below this one. I thought it was Figel. But it was Miguel. I asked what he was doing there. He said he was collecting souvernirs of Figel, because Figel was dead. Then he told me that there had been a lot of shooting, on the houseboat. He advised me to stay in Amsterdam, and asked whether I needed money. When I said no, he left, with Figel's four cigar boxes under his arm. I looked all over Figel's room, but I couldn't find it. Was there anything on the boat, in the small wall cupboard in the bedroom? A flat brown bottle?"

"No, there was nothing at all. What did Miguel say about me?"

"He said that you had got away in the general confusion."

She begins to moan again. I must keep her thoughts occupied till the tablet starts to take effect. I ask:

"How did you get the habit? From Figel?"

She raises her eyes to me and now she really sees me, for she says:

"You don't look too good, either." She casts a quick glance into the small travelling mirror propped up against the wall, and she pushes the sticky lock away from her forehead.   Then she says bitterly:

"No, the mess I am in is all of my own making.   It began two years ago, when I was still foolish enough to think I could get an engagement in a really good nightclub.   The managers were very, very kind to me, but they are business-men and they kept business and pleasure strictly apart.   The mornings after I felt like hell, and a boy friend from the West Indies gave me doctored cigarettes.   Then I met Figel, and he gave me the real stuff."

She bites her lip, suppressing a cry of pain.

"What are you going to do now that Figel is dead?"

"Get somewhere a good supply of the stuff and leave Holland.   Figel gave me my boat ticket, and a hundred American dollars."

"Figel seems to have been a generous fellow."

"He was.   The money he used to give me went a long way to make both ends meet for me and the regular boy-friend I was staying with.   Bert never knew it came from Figel, of course.   He thought I got it at Chez Claude.   Chez Claude, of all places!   The pittance I got there wouldn't have kept me in nylons.   Where was I?"

"You were talking about your plans for the future."

"Oh yes.   Well, I shall go to Beirut, and stay with Figel's wife, for a while."

"Stay with his wife?"

She shrugs and says:

"Forget that story I told you about Figel having arranged a tour for me through the Middle East.   And also what I said about sending him my picture.   I told you all that non-sense only in order to see your reactions.   I thought you were from the police, you see. And I was afraid that you would make me miss this chance of leaving Amsterdam."

"What was your hurry?"

"I was afraid that Bert, my regular boy-friend, would find out that I am a drug addict. The boy thinks the world of me, believe it or not. Every time I needed the drug, I would tell him that I had to do a turn up country, or so, and I went to stay on Figel's boat, for a day or two. I had the key, and the stuff was in the wall cupboard in the bedroom, so that was all right, even if Figel wasn't there. But when I began to need it nearly every other day, I knew that Bert would find out. He's still a boy, in many ways, but he's by no means a fool. Well, I told Figel that I wanted to go away, and he said that suited him fine because he had to return to Beirut in a day or two, and that I could go with him. On a ship called the "Djibouty", bound for Alexandria."

"What did Figel do for a living?"

"Oh, a bit of everything. He traded in cars, electrical appliances, tobacco. He also set up bars and nightclubs, and sold them again after he had made them run. He owned one in Beirut, and he said I could do a turn there, perhaps. He was a Pole, originally, but he spent his entire life in the Middle East. He made business trips to Europe regularly, and Amsterdam was his headquarters. His wife is also from Poland, a Jewess, he told me, and the Nazis caught her. Made her an army-whore and treated her so badly that her mind got deranged and she's woolgathering half of the time, the poor thing. Oh for Heaven's sake, that awful rain has started again."

While listening silently to the clatter of the downpour on the roof I reflect that only a few facts tally with what I overheard when Achmad was telling Mochtar about Figel's antecedents. What Achmad said was evidently the truth. Figel had to tell Eveline that he had been in the Middle East all his life, because he couldn't well own to his having been a Nazi-leader; and one who took part in drawing up the program for the extermination of the Jews too. It must have been a big surprise to Figel when he discovered that his own sweetheart, the Jewish girl from Poland, had been subjected to the inhuman, cruel treatment he himself had helped to devise. I reflect that if Figel hadn't been a Nazi associating with mass-murderers, he would have been a rather pathetic person.

"This downpour can't last long," I remark.

She gets a crumpled package of cigarettes out of her coat pocket, lights one and throws the empty package into the corner.

"Figel wasn't such a bad fellow to get along with," she says pensively. "He was very fond of his wife. The house in Beirut stands in her name, and he has put a lot of money for her in the bank. She knows about her husband and me, and she'll let me stay there. That means that I'll have a roof over my head, at least."

"I thought you said that Figel was so fond of his wife. Why did he then . . ."

"He was," she interrupts impatiently. "But she being weak-minded, and having been in the hands of the Nazi camp-doctors, well, you know what I mean. Figel did without for a long time, it seems. Then he met me, and he grew fond of me, after a fashion."

"Why then did he give you drugs, instead of helping you to get rid of the habit?"

"Because he wanted to sleep with me only when I was drugged and he was drunk. That way it was so far remote from the real thing, he said, that it wouldn't make him a

108

complete cad. He had it all worked out for himself, you see. And it cured me nicely of my tiresome self-respect. Anyway, I'll stay with Figel's wife, and see what will turn up."

"Staying with Figel's widow will get you into trouble," I say.

"Why?"

"Because Figel and the two Egyptians were working for a man in Cairo, a very tough old party, from what I heard. When his three agents don't come back on the "Djibouty", he'll wonder what happened to them, and he'll send out a couple of unpleasant characters to investigate. Figel's Beirut address will be on their list, and you'd better not be there when they come to call. Have you got no relatives here you could go to?"

She shakes her head, determinedly. Now that the tablet has soothed the pain, her old spirit is coming back.

"My parents died when I was only fourteen, and I was brought up by my elder sister. That rat of a husband of hers used to bother me and both were glad when I was eighteen and they could wash their hands of me. I don't want to go there, and they wouldn't have me. Never."

"In that case, I'd go back to Bert. I read the letter he wrote you, and I think he's very fond of you. I only wonder why he sent you a letter, instead of coming here to talk it over with you." A regular little Captain Uyeda, I am. But I want everything neat and orderly. Eveline doesn't mind.

"I hadn't told him this address, so as to prevent him from doing that. He sent his letter care of Figel, to Chez Claude. I didn't want Bert to know when and how I would be leaving Amsterdam." She thinks for a while, I see the deep lines by the side of her full mouth. "No, I couldn't possibly go back to Bert, I have made trouble enough for him already. His parents are the strict, religious type, you see. They didn't object to me as artiste, not too much, that is, and neither to a student marriage, as long as it was a real marriage, mind you. When I went to live with Bert without wedding bells, they disowned the poor fellow, and stopped his allowance."

"Bert didn't want to marry you?"

"Of course he wanted to marry me! But don't you see that I had to say no? If I had met him when I was still on the cigarettes only, I'd have said yes. Settling down as a steady small Amsterdam housewife wasn't exactly my idea of fun, but who can tell whether fun's so funny, after all? Anyway, I met Bert two months after Figel had taken me on. Just my bad luck. Have you got a cigarette? I am through mine." After I have given her one and lit it for her, she draws on it deeply.

"My idea was," she continues wearily, "to write to Bert from Beirut later, telling him that I wouldn't come back because I had met a very fine chap and married him. Bert would have been sad for a while, but he would have got over that, and then everything would be all right for him again. I am no saint, as you'll have discovered by now, but I draw the line at messing up other people's lives."

"Many men like a woman messing up their life for them," I say. "It makes them feel important. And every man likes to feel important."

"Maybe. But Bert is too young for that. Breaking with his parents was an awful wrench, for he and his mother were very close. He is not like you and me, you see. He is desperately serious. He would never have carried on with me without church and registry if I hadn't told him that we would get to that in due time, when both of us were quite sure. He is always trying to figure things out for himself, you know, worrying about what's happening to the world and all that.

I didn't mind listening to him, for I liked his voice, and it's nice to listen to a chap who really means what he says, for a change. If Bert would come to know me for what I really am, he would kill himself. Believe it or not."

"I don't agree with you at all. Bert being that kind of a chap, he'd love to raise a fallen woman, as they call it in the books Bert read at home. I think you should tell him everything. Skipping only the bit about bedding with Figel, of course. Honesty is like charity in that it's most effective when dealt out judiciously."

She gives me a nasty look.

"You'll never understand a nice, straightforward youngster like Bert. And I am not going to say thank you for the rest of my life anyway. Not to anybody, and certainly not to Bert." She bites her lip. Then she gives me a searching look and says curtly: " You would take me, if I was agreeable, you said earlier tonight. Does that offer still stand?"

"Of course."

"Well," she says with a bleak smile, "in that case you might tell me something more about yourself. I said that before, but I mean it this time, literally! Aren't you married?"

"I have been, twice. Both my wives have died."

"Tell me about them, if you don't mind. That'll give me a general idea about what you are like yourself." She stubs out her cigarette. "I am going to lie down, though."

She gets up and shakes the housecoat from her shoulders. Her pyjama jacket is drenched with perspiration.

I quickly fold the padded quilt back for her and she gets underneath. Stretching herself out on her belly, she puts her head on her folded arms, on the pillow. I cover her up with the quilt, and lay the housecoat on top. Then I sit back and light myself a new cigarette. The rain has stopped, it is very quiet now. After a while I say:

"There was a time when I thought I was responsible for their deaths, both of them. It was all rather confused, you see. My second wife was called Lina, and she looked exactly like you. She..."

"Did she love you?"

"At times, yes. For the rest, I am not too sure. My first wife, Effie as I called her, was a nice level-headed girl, of my own sort. We went to Java, and we had a small daughter. I was fond of my wife and she of me. But I was a fool, I thought that our life together was too smooth and placid, not romantic enough for being the real thing. Not... not violent enough, if you get what I mean."

"No, I don't get it at all," she says crossly.

I don't get it myself, quite. So I say: "It doesn't matter, really. Well, it's many a year ago, in 1942. When you were two years old, as a matter of fact. My daughter Bubu was four." I give her a brief outline of the Jap landings on Java, and the confused situation. "I had been made a captain, and I had been rushing about in my jeep for twenty-four hours. I ended up in Bandong, helping our troops to maintain some sort of order there during the Jap air raids. In my own district up country native fanatics were on the rampage, and I was worried about my wife. But not too much, for she had always done a lot for the natives, and they respected her. Also, I knew that our servants were loyal. At ten at night the colonel told me I could go home, an hour's drive through the countryside. I stopped in a small hotel on the outskirts of the town, for a quick beer. That's where you came in. Only your name was Lina. Some drunken soldiers had got into a quarrel about her, and..."

"Was she a streetwalker?"

"No, she was not. She was available, if you know what I mean. Well, one of the soldiers went berserk and wanted to kill her. I shot him and slept with her. Not exactly the right thing to do. The sleeping bit, I mean."

She shrugs her shoulders.

"It just gets you that way, sometimes. I know."

"Right. I went on one hour later, and thought it had all been for the best, after all, for a jeep with a platoon of military police overtook me, and I told them to escort me. We ran into an ambush, my jeep got smashed up but the soldiers drove the attackers off, and gave me a lift home. The incident meant another half hour lost. When I came home, our house was on fire. The religious fanatics had attacked one hour earlier and slaughtered my wife, my small daughter and our native servants."

I draw on my cigarette and resume:

"In the overwrought condition I was in, the shock did for me. When I came to, delirious, I was a prisoner of the Japs. They were dragging me along to Bandong, because they had been looking for another man called Hendriks, one of our intelligence agents and they thought I was him. So they wanted to question me. Are you asleep?"

"No, I am listening. Tell me more about Lina."

"Later I heard that Lina had rushed out there when she heard about the massacre, the next morning. After I had passed out, the fanatics had come back and killed the four soldiers that had been with me. Me they left lying there for dead. Lina found me and nursed me, and when the Japs came she told them to let their medics give me a couple of shots, persuading them that you can't question a dead man. She had a way with her, Lina. I was in the camp and in the military police prison for more than three years, but she was free, because she was half-Indonesian, you see. She visited me regularly, smuggling in useful things for me. When the war was over, I married her. Not out of gratitude, mind you. Just because I wanted her, terribly."

"She'll have liked that better than your gratitude," Eveline remarks dryly. "How did it work out?"

I tell her a bit about our years together, and then how she was shot dead by our former houseboy. Eveline remains silent so long that I bend over her to see whether she has fallen asleep. I wouldn't blame her. But she is wide awake. She turns her head round to me and says:

"Of course she loved you. Else she wouldn't have visited you for three years. Three years is a very long time, in a young girl's life. The child was yours, and you were responsible for her death. Not for that of your first wife, that was just rotten luck. If you had left town earlier, those fellows who were lying in ambush would have killed you. And if they had missed you, the people who attacked your house would have got you."

"No, that ambush had been there only twenty minutes or so. We questioned one of their wounded, and he could tell us that, just before he kicked the bucket. And as regards those fanatics, I had known their leader quite well. He used to visit me to discuss all kinds of religious problems, and I would quote from their holy book, in the original Arabic. That means a lot to those people, you know. They were in a frenzy when they attacked, but I could have made them see reason, I think. If I had been there to talk to them, that is."

She shrugs again.

"Have it you own way. But, as to your second wife, her you killed all right. For you wished that she were dead. And that is a damned nasty thing to do."

"I couldn't agree more."

She props up her pillow against the wall, turns over and sits up with her back against it. She draws up her legs and pulls the quilt over them. Then she says bitterly:

"Yes, I have got it now. You keep running after me not because you like me, but because to you I am part and parcel of that damned complex of yours. You take a hell of a lot for granted where women are concerned, my friend." She shakes her head and goes on in a resigned voice: "The trouble with us women is that we pass by the real nice, simple chaps who'll take out time to consider what we feel and think, sometimes. And so we get stuck with utterly selfish fellows like you and Figel, who don't care a damn about us and who brood over their own complexes like a hen over its eggs." She shrugs her shoulders. "Maleesh, it can't be helped, as Figel used to say. Well, where were you thinking of taking me? I can't stay with you here in Amsterdam, for I don't want to run into Bert."

I put my elbows on my knees, cup my chin in my hands, and look at her. It strikes me that, sitting hunched up like that, I must resemble Captain Uyeda, studying a prisoner. Not as impersonally, though. She still is a very desirable woman to me. And it might be argued that although my mental outlook has changed completely these last few hours, the routine of life will go on, has to go on. I must eat and drink, and walk and sleep, and presumably have a woman by my side. For all the Zen texts are agreed that a balanced mind requires a balanced body. I could help Eveline to regain her balance too, even. 'Re-integrating the addict into normal society" — that was the title of the last chapter of my O.R.S.-report. "The author is aware of the Government's moral responsibilities," a high official in Batavia noted approvingly in the margin. I was pleased as Punch, at the time. I am not so pleased now. Renouncing is difficult. Even if one has ascended the top of Mount Fuji. But I ought to make a clean break with my life here in Amsterdam anyway. It has become a city of shadows to me. A dead city, where I would for ever be alone.

"Did Figel fix your passport all right?"

When she nods, I shake out a second tablet from the tin tube, and lay it on the suitcase, by the plastic beaker.

"You need a good rest," I say. "Take this second tablet, it will make you sleep till late in the morning. I'll pick you up, and we'll have a good luncheon, together. Then we drive off, in my old car, to Paris. There we'll hunt out a place where we can buy a supply of the stuff, so that you can taper it off. Then we go farther south, to the Mediterranean, say Southern Spain. Lie on the beach, do a bit of swimming and boating. I need a long holiday myself, and I have funds to see us through for half a year or so. Thereafter we'll see what we do next." I rather like that. I don't like what I have to add, but it's part of the cure. "You needn't say thank you to me, not even once. For I always like to have a woman of my own around when I am on a holiday, and your coming along will save me the bother and the money of finding in a hurry one that suits me."

She doesn't like that one, but she takes it like a brick.

"That seems a very good idea," she says calmly. "I have never been farther south than Brussels, and it'll be fun to see what they are wearing in Paris. Will you come here to fetch me?"

"I'd better not. There were some difficulties with Miguel, tonight, and the police might be keeping an eye on this house, tomorrow. You'd better leave by the garden gate. Let's meet on the Dam, say at the War Monument. There are lots of good eating places nearby. I shall be there at quarter to two, with my car." I get up. She stretches out her hand from under the quilt. I squeeze it, and it is small and warm.

"See you on the Dam!" she says with a bleak little smile.

I pull the door shut behind me and go down the narrow stairs. On the landing I halt by the newel with the Janus head, and I have a closer look at his two faces. Both are smiling. Smiling at the coming in and at the going out. I have decided to go out, definitely. So I have two faces too, one is smiling, the other is looking sour. Which of them is right? I sigh and consult my watch. It's half past five. An early morning. I pat Janus on his wooden curls and descend the broad staircase.

I walk about at random in the dark streets, turning corners till I see what I am looking for. Namely a public telephone in its neat glass cell. I take out my wallet and consult the old bill. Then I put my ten-cent piece into the slot, and dial five times eight. A fairly alert voice answers nearly at once. I don't pay my taxes entirely for nothing, apparently. I clear my throat importantly and say:

"I have some information for you. There's a hotel or boarding house somewhere on the Zeeburgerdyk, phone number doublenine-oh-six-four ... Have you got that? No, this is not a practical joke. Definitely not. No, I don't know the name, but I repeat the phone number: doublenine-oh-six-four. A foreigner staying there has in his possession four cigar boxes containing illicit drugs. The man's personal name is Miguel. Yes, I'll spell that. M of Michael, I of Isaac ... You can't miss him, tall, fair, curly hair, small fair moustache. I am not sure he knows that the boxes contain drugs, mind you. They may have been foisted on him, by an international smuggling gang. Their headquarters are in Cairo, I think. Good luck and good-bye." I hang up on his excited questions.

I am not a policeman, but I am the author of the O.R.S.-report. I put a lot of research into that, visited hospitals and clinics and saw the human wrecks there. And I just left Eveline. If I can help it, that large shipment won't reach its destination. I wonder, however, why I gave Miguel the benefit of the doubt. Probably because I have a feeling that he saved me from getting my head kicked in.

I cross the street, deep in thought. A butcherboy on his bike swerves at the last moment and he misses me.

"Watch your step, you oaf!" he shouts over his shoulder.

He's right, I'd better watch my step. I don't know whether the police can trace calls from a public telephone. While I am looking for a taxi I try to sort out the facts. Miguel is a shrewd fellow, he cleverly played on my interest in Eveline to fortify me in my mistaken notion that Figel and his men were white-slavers. They weren't. They were dealers in illicit drugs; less risky, and twenty times more profitable. They had just completed a fruitful tour of Europe. Since Achmad spoke to Mochtar about buying and selling, they must have sold the local product of Egypt, for instance opium or hemp, and bought heroine, cocaine or some other blessings of our modern Western civilization. On behalf of that venerable old fellow in Cairo whom they referred to as the Sheikh. The fact that Achmad mentioned selling should have told me that I was on the wrong track in taking them for white slavers. I had too many other things on my mind then, evidently.

Michael doesn't deal in white slaves nor in illicit drugs. I believe he is indeed a gigolo and occasional jewel thief, as he told me. Figel took him on because Miguel is at home in the capitals and pleasure resorts of Western Europe, and thus would be able to introduce Figel to the right people. As a reward for services rendered, Figel had promised to get Miguel to Egypt, and to supply him there with a new passport and a new identity.

All this I have got straight now. Also the first phase of what happened on the houseboat. Mochtar was a professional killer who lost his nerve when he had to kill the one man he secretly admired. In a frenzy he wanted then to kill everybody in sight, and me in the first place. Figel wanted to intervene, and he shot Figel. I can't believe Mochtar and Figel shot each other dead practically simultaneously, Miguel must have borrowed that idea from some dime-novel or other. I believe that Miguel came inside directly behind Figel, and not after an interval, as he told me; that part of his story was pretty weak, for who cares how he parks a car on a lonely quay in the deep of night? Miguel saw Mochtar shooting Figel, and Miguel shot Mochtar before Mochtar could shoot him too. Miguel is no killer, he shot Mochtar in self-defense. After Miguel had shot Mochtar, he realized that the shipment of drugs, worth a small fortune, was there for the taking, for he was the only one left now. He had known all along that the drugs were concealed in the cigar boxes, hence his elaborate play-acting with the cigar case he took from Figel's pocket. For Figel's cigars were very much on his mind then. I don't believe Miguel deliberately shot both Mochtar and Figel in order to get the drugs all to himself. But that is exactly what the police would think, after they would have traced Figel's activities, and found out that he didn't traffic in women, but in drugs. Hence Miguel's eagerness to have me tell them my story. And he will have seen to it that the facts supported that story, putting the right pistols in the right places so as to fit the right bullets. He had plenty of time to arrange all that, while I was lying there with my face to the wall, half-stunned.

The odds are that the police nab Miguel in his hostel. He told me that he would phone them in three or four hours, suggesting that he was about to leave Holland in Figel's car, and make his call from a frontier station. But that was only to pull the wool over my eyes. Why should he leave Holland with his precious four boxes? International drug rings have a splendid organization, so he would risk getting the Sheikh's European agents on his heels, not to speak of the French police. The "Djibouty" is out, of course, for that good ship belongs to the Sheikh. Amsterdam isn't a bad city to get lost in, for a while, provided you have the money and you speak the language. In due time Miguel could contact here an agent of one of the Sheikh's rivals, get rid of the stuff, and clear out.

Miguel is a slick customer, he knows exactly how to make his lies convincing by adding a modicum of truth. He may be able to persuade the police that he didn't know the cigar boxes contained illicit drugs. He has Figel's papers and Achmad's notebook, so he'll be able to supply the police with a long list of very interesting names and addresses, and the police will be duly grateful. He'll tell them a long story, but he'll carefully refrain from mentioning the houseboat, Eveline or me. He was staying in the vicinity, so he must have heard the explosion, and have gone to have a look at the damage. He'll have reached the conclusion that I had been killed, and that he is responsible. So he'll keep mum on all that, for he's a clever scoundrel. That Eveline surprised him when he came back all the way to Abelstraat 53 just to fetch a supply of cigars he doesn't smoke, and that Eveline mentioned that to me, was just his bad luck. He may yet get round to his solitary fishing in St. Georges Bay, or in the bay of Naples. If he keeps his hands off the jewelry of his middle-aged girl friends, and if his faulty heart doesn't let him down.

I hear voices ahead. They sound very loud in the still street. Two drunks are arguing with a cab-driver, under a street-lamp. When I have strolled up to them I hear that the motor is running. I give a sign to the driver and step inside. We drive off, leaving the two drunks standing on the curb, still cursing. Loudly, but without imagination.

As we are rounding the corner the driver says:

"I don't mind their being drunk. I like a drop myself, off-duty. But they oughtn't to call me no names. What number did you say again?"

I give him the number, and he drives me home.

THE TRYST ON THE DAM

After I have opened the familiar brown front door with my latchkey, I walk on to the wall telephone in the chilly hall, and consult the dog-eared directory. Nivas Ltd. is listed, just as I thought. There won't be any difficulty there, for one doesn't stir out of one's room when one has a real hangover. I jot the number down on the wall which is decorated already by the phone-numbers and hieroglyphic designs scribbled there by my fellow-boarders.

The next item poses a problem. About two years ago, a doctor here in Amsterdam wrote to me as the author of the O.R.S.-report, asking for some additional details, since he was specializing in the curing of drug addicts. It was a very nice letter, but I never replied to it, and now I can't think of his name. I grab the classified directory and scan the long list of doctors. Suddenly I recognize his name, among the neurologists. I write that on the wall too, then I go upstairs. On tiptoe, for the shoddy stair-carpet is threadbare, and I don't want to startle my old landlady. I enjoy the reputation of a quiet, steady lodger.

I switch on the light in my bed-sitting room. It has two windows facing the street, now concealed behind the long curtains of dark-green serge. The room is cold and dreary, and I quickly step up to the pot-bellied stove, open the shutter of the pipe, and rattle the grate vigorously till a few glowing coals are coming down. I stand myself in front of the stove, my back towards the wooden chimney that is painted so as to resemble spotted marble.

My hands thrusted deep into the pockets of my mackintosh I critically survey my cheap desk of painted wood, and the upholstered armchair behind it with the ugly tear in the leather I planned to have mended but never did. My day-bed, chaste and narrow, under the wooden shelf I nailed on the wall for putting my alarm-clock and my small radio on. The iron stand with the gas-cooker where I make tea and coffee. The set of bookshelves I bought· on an auction, loaded with the books I bought one by one but none of which proved of lasting advantage to me. And the too large wardrobe, willed to my landlady by her deceased cousin. Or was it her aunt?

It was the continuous presence of the past that vested this room with an intimate atmosphere all its own. Now that the links with the past have been severed, it has become empty and meaningless. I suddenly shiver. I must have caught a bad cold, over on the houseboat. As soon as the room has warmed up, I shall undress, put on my bathrobe, and have a long, hot shower in the shower-cell, on the landing. Then I shall set the alarm-clock at quarter to one, and go to bed. Seven hours of solid sleep.

I do have the long, hot shower, and I do have the long sleep, seven hours of it without dreams. But when the alarm wakes me, I find I have a dull headache, and my entire body feels so stiff and sore that I doubt whether I can get up at all. After a few false starts I do get up, however, I turn the radio on, and fetch my medicine-box from the wardrobe. Stripped naked I pull my chair close to the stove that is burning red-hot now. I begin to put ointment on the assorted bruises and sore spots my body is covered with, to the accompaniment of the news-broadcast. When the police bulletin starts, I stop and listen. Presently I hear:

This morning police-officers found an unusually large amount of illicit drugs on an Argentine national called M.F. who is staying in a boarding-house in the harbour quarter. The drugs were concealed in Havana cigars, individually packed in aluminium tubes, in four boxes containing fifty cigars each. The drugs are believed to belong to a foreign smuggling ring and to be destined for the Middle East. The police are holding the said M.F., for questioning.

There follows a list of misdemeanours and minor thefts, and I concentrate on my sore ribs. There doesn't seem to be any serious damage. I am fairly tough. Captain Uyeda said so, and he knew what he was talking about. It's my emotional life that is weak and confused. Was weak and confused, I should say, rather. I prick up my ears again. The announcer is broadcasting local mishaps and accidents in his customary genial voice. The item I am waiting for is brief but to the point:

A few hours before dawn a houseboat moored at the end of the Nieuwevaart caught fire. There was a severe explosion and although the firebrigade was there within a commendable brief space of time they could not prevent the boat from burning out completely. It is believed no one was on board at the time of the accident but the investigation is still in progress. The boat was registered in the name of Dr. Armand Klaussner of Egyptian nationality, present address unknown.

The announcer spells the name, then requests the said Dr. Klaussner to communicate at his early convenience with a well-known insurance agency. I get up with a sigh of satisfaction and turn the radio off.

I dress quickly and go downstairs. My landlady is at the telephone, engaged in an involved discussion with the butcher-shop. At last she hangs up and tells me that there'll be a nice porkchop for dinner. When she has ambled off to the kitchen, I dial the number of Nivas Ltd. and politely ask the chap who answers to call Mr. Winter from his room in the basement. After a minute or two I hear Bert's voice. He gravely inquires who is speaking.

"Hendriks" I say. "I had an appointment with Eveline on the Dam, at quarter to two. Will you please tell her that there were complications and that I can't make it? You'll find her on the Dam, in front of the War Monument. At quarter to two. Tell her I am sorry, will you, and wish her good luck. No, she isn't leaving Amsterdam. Yes, she's all right. But she discovered that Figel is a cad, after all, and she's a bit overwrought. Get her to go and see Dr. . . . ." I give him the name of the neurologist I have written on the wall. Eveline will get the hint. She can tell Bert all about it, later. After a couple of years or so. "What did you say? Oh, I met her at Chez Claude once. Hendriks is my name. Yes, quarter to two. If she shouldn't be there at two, give me a ring, will you?" I give him my number and hang up.

Then I dial the number of my office. The present has been liquidated and the future disowned, but the routine of life goes on. I tell the fellow in charge that I woke up with a bad cold, but that I'll try to come in later in the afternoon.

I go up to my room again, lie down on my bed fully dressed as I am, and turn on the radio, very soft. There's a good concert on and I listen, my mind a blank. At quarter past two the performance is over. I turn the radio off. Bert hasn't phoned, so my performance is over too.

I get up, fill the kettle from the tap in the wash-basin, and put it on the gas-cooker. While waiting for the water to boil, I stare sourly at the oil-painting on the wall above the stand. It's a clumsy still-life, a vase filled with too bright flowers, and the vase is not in perspective. I hate the thing, but I could never summon the courage to ask my landlady to remove it, for it was willed to her, together with the unwieldy wardrobe, by her dead cousin. Or aunt. I tell myself to make first a cup of good strong tea, and then a few slices of toast.

It is as if I were telling someone else to do those things. Does it really matter, though, whether I make tea and toast, or someone else? It doesn't, really. For I am non-existent. A man who has dissolved the links with his past, has liquidated the present, and disowned the future, that man is in fact non-existent. This bit of reasoning is quite all right. But I am not all right. A terrible, hollow feeling is rising in my breast.

Suddenly I see myself as I am standing there in front of the gas-cooker, my hands clasped behind my back, shoulders bent, head thrust forward. No, it isn't I. It's Captain Uyeda. He is standing over me, waiting. Waiting till I shall come down from the ascent of Mount Fuji. He can wait as long as he likes. I can taunt him now, that small man with the large spectacles. Tell him that I shall not come down, never. That I have reached the summit and that I shall breathe forever the pure, still air of that frozen height. And then the strange thing happens. At the very moment that I am telling him this, exultantly, I suddenly know that what I am saying is not true, for I do want to come down. Down from the summit, and back to him. But I can't see Uyeda any more, he has left. I am all alone now. All alone amidst the eternal snow. This is the very last sensation I shall have, that of utter loneliness. Presently my being will evaporate into the still blue air, and I shall have ceased to exist.

I am afraid, and I want to go down. I want to go down, down to Uyeda whom I hanged, and down to Figel, Achmad and Mochtar whom I burned. I want to go down to them, desperately, before my being disintegrates. For I don't want to be alone, I do want to exist. I want to share their anguish and their perplexities because I am they and they are me. I long for them, I want to be with them, they are the only valid reason why I am I. Without them I am lost.

And then I feel that the eternal snow is melting.

It's getting warmer around me, warm air makes the snow melt. It rises and strokes my cheeks. The hard, azure sky is changing into a blurred, comfortable gray. I open my eyes, and I heave a deep sigh of immense relief. I am standing bent over the kettle, my hands pressed against the wall for support. Under the clumsy still-life with the too bright flowers and the vase that is not in perspective. The steam from the kettle is curling up into my face.

I step back. And suddenly I smile. At long last I, Johan Hendriks, have defeated Captain Uyeda Morisada. I have defeated him, and for ever. Because I have recognized myself in him, and have identified myself with him. A deep, humble gratitude is spreading its warm comfort all through my being.

I shall have to proceed now with the utmost care, step by step, so as not to lose this again, this unbelievable gift that has been bestowed upon me. Let me be careful, then, and use Uyeda's terminology, for a while. Uyeda had achieved the complete detachment of the frozen summit when he was still young, in Kyoto; many years before me who reached it only early this morning, on the houseboat. The detachment that is technically called Emptiness, the emptiness of all purpose and all desire. But Uyeda had come to a halt after that, he had been puzzling about the next and final step ever after, without being able to find it. And yet it is so simple, all the texts state it so clearly: after the complete detachment from the world, there must come the complete reidentification, technically designated as Compassion. Emptiness and Compassion, the two key-terms which Uyeda knew so well yet could not understand, just as I knew the key-terms of my own world, and yet never understood them. When Uyeda's Zenmaster in Kyoto found that his pupil could not find the final answer, he sent him away. But to me the answer was granted, on this twenty-ninth of February, this given day. Granted to me who wilfully went away and who was yet allowed to come back.

The common divisor has been laid into my hands, and with this I now dare to approach the terms of my own Christian world. Terms so familiar that we take them for granted, even abuse them in common parlance; terms so well known indeed that it is hard, very hard to realize their full meaning. And I marvel at the endless compassion shown to us who never deserved it and shall never deserve it, because, since times immemorial, we have persistently misused and wantonly squandered all that was given to us while yet clamouring for more. The astonishing fact that, as a wholly unmerited favour, we are still allowed to exist, is an irrefutable act of Mercy. Of a Mercy so overwhelming and all-pervading that even the merest glimpse of it will suffice to make us partake of the grace of believing.

Effie, Lina, forgive me. Forgive me for not having loved you enough when you were here, and for persistently trying to drag you down from where you are now, down to my utterly selfish worries. And you too, Bubu, forgive me for wishing you to be always near me, even though I myself used to warn you never to stray from your home. Forgive me, as I am forgiven, for look, as a wholly unmerited favour the dissolved past, the liquidated present and the disowned future have been given back to me.

I turn the gas-cooker down and go to the window. When I have drawn the curtains, I see that the bleak midday sun of this late winter is deepening the gray of the street and the houses into a tender beige. I hear the laughter of the children playing on the curb, and the excited voices of two girls who pass by hand in hand. And somewhere round the corner a barrel-organ is playing a tune I had forgotten. I am part of all this, part of this living city I love and where I shall never again be alone.

NOTES

Page   73   The quotation at the head of the chapter is found in the second *sura* of the Quran, verse 286.

Page   80   Jeruzalem is holy to the Muhammedans because tradition has it that the Prophet Muhammad there ascended to Heaven.

The "Chapter of the Elephant" is the 105th *sura* of the Quran.   "Companions of the Elephant" refers to the Ethiopians who attacked Mecca ca. 570 A.D. but were destroyed by a miracle.

"Saving your presence".   The speaker has to apologize before bringing up the subject of the sandals, because footwear is one of the traditional Arab unmentionables.   Sandals and shoes are vaguely associated with unclean things and death.

Page 122   The seventh blueprint was suggested by the most accomplished *yantra* (mystic chart) of the Yoga system, the so-called *Shri-yantra*.   Cf. plate 36 of Heinrich Zimmer, *Myths and symbols of Indian Art and Civilization*, New York 1947 (The Bollingen Series vol. VI).

Page 129   Zen represents the flower of Sino-Indian and Japanese thought.   It is often referred to as a religious or philosophical system.   Zen is neither.   It is a method for reaching salvation — a method that can not be learned from books but only from life itself. It culminates in sudden enlightenment (Chinese *tun-wu*, Japanese *satori*), the awakening to a new world of ultimate reality where all values have fundamentally changed. As a rule this unique experience just happens to one. However, the Zen-master may help the disciple by confronting him with a pointed question or terse remark, a "Zen-problem", technically called *kung-an* (Japanese *ko-an*). The phrase regarding the snow on Mount Fuji is an example of such a *kung-an*. Since Zen is essentially a method, it is of universal application. In this novel it is the bridge by which the main person returns to his own Christian creed. For an excellent introduction to Zen cf. Alan W. Watts, *The Spirit of Zen*, John Murray London 1955.

"Emptiness" (Sanskrit *Shunyata*) and "Compassion" (Sanskrit *Karuna*) are the two key-terms of Tantrism, the final development of Mahayana Buddhism, which greatly influenced Zen in its initial Chinese phase. "Emptiness" is described as the static, negative state of Perfected Knowledge which separates him who has achieved it from the world of suffering. "Compassion" acts as a dynamic, positive impulse that causes him to re-identify himself with the world and all living beings.

ROBERT VAN GULIK
The Hague, Jan., 1963.

POSTSCRIPT

Dr. Robert van Gulik is mainly known by his 'Chinese' novels, a series of seventeen short and longer thrillers featuring Judge Dee, an antique magistrate of the T'ang Dynasty (618-907). Van Gulik, a brilliant and internationally famous sinologue, lived from 1910 to 1967. His studies earned him a *summa cum laude* Ph.D. in Far Eastern Literature at the age of 24 (Universities of Leyden and Utrecht) on a dissertation called *The Horse Cult of China, Tibet, India and Japan*. A most unusual scholar had emerged, fluent in many modern and ancient languages, with interests in law, medicine, music, art, history and the bizarre. Scholars are often cloistered in universities, chained to their desks. Van Gulik preferred movement and became a diplomat, representing the Netherlands in East Africa, Egypt, India, China, the United States, the Lebanon, Malaya and, at the beginning and end of his career, Japan. He was born, and died, in Holland, and spent time there in between, first as a schoolboy and student and later as a high official employed by the Foreign Ministry.

We may presume, when we peruse his work, that China and things Chinese were Van Gulik's main interest. The Judge Dee mysteries, based on plots gained from ancient textbooks for the instruction of Imperial Judges, are masterpieces of carefully reconstructed living history. The Dee mysteries became textbooks in their own right, published by the University of Chicago, but the material is so fascinating that all volumes in the series are today, thirty years after they were written, available in the racks of most commercial bookstores.

'I am Dee,' Van Gulik was heard to say when, bored by the fashionable cocktail parties of diplomats, he withdrew within the company of literary friends. And maybe he was. Chinese scholars saw the tall, wide-shouldered foreigner who looked somewhat—his contemporaries claimed—like an intellectual buccaneer,' as a reincarnation of their own kind, forgave him his heavy Dutch accent, and called him Kao Lo Pei (高 羅 佩), a pen name Van Gulik subsequently used for his many Chinese publications.

All of us wear different masks. The Greek word for mask is *persona*. The more evolved we become the more masks we can use to hide behind. Van Gulik also assumed an Arabic personality and mastered that language while he taught, as a guest professor, at the University of Beirut. He studied the Koran, enjoyed the spiritual and learned company of bewhiskered sheiks, wandered through the bazaars, eavesdropped on the terraces of coffeehouses and, as was his wont, found small printing shops where he helped (he liked to stain his hands with ink) to have some of his writings published.

In order to stretch his available time he managed to suffice with little sleep and studied at night while he worked and observed during the day.

In China and Japan Van Gulik aimed to penetrate the secrets of Zen and Taoism, staying well away from monastic limitations and the ignorant ramblings of greedy gurus. In the U.S. he visited libraries and museums, benefiting from the vast stored wealth of a well organized and powerful country. In Malaya he traveled in the interior, and in India he would be lost for weeks, on semi-private errands that infuriated his superiors who were no match for him.

Van Gulik wrote on the Chinese seven-stringed lute (that he played), the Gibbon monkeys (that he kept), Chinese Pictorial Art (that he collected and practiced) and Chinese Ancient Sexual Life (by hearsay from literature and art). His main work was published by the presses of famous universities.

So what did he publish himself, in those quaint shops, usually primitively equipped? Short stories that Van Gulik gave away, neatly bound, as New Year presents, erotic tales that he presented to special friends, essays that he distributed to libraries and one complete novel, *The Given Day*.

The Given Day is a rare book, amidst the profusion of scholarly work that streamed from Van Gulik's pen and brush, and it deals with a rare quality of his own character, his Dutchness, the lesser aspect of a many-sided personality, brought about by the genes received from physical parents. Van Gulik, for once, identified with a countryman, the Mr. Hendriks you followed in the previous pages.

Van Gulik wrote and published this Amsterdam-set drama in 1964, three years before his death. The English version was privately published in Kuala Lumpur. He had been the Netherlands ambassador there and was about to rise even higher. When he died he was the Dutch ambassador to Japan, a cherished post in present diplomacy—for isn't Japan a key factor in the mutual development of East and West? But wasn't Japan also a source of evil, not so long ago? Van Gulik was in Japan when World War II started, saw the impact of the sneak attack on Pearl Harbor, lived through the fascist egotism that corrupted his hosts, evacuated to China where, in Chungking, Zero airplanes kept bombing and strafing civilians. Japan caused daily havoc in Van Gulik's life, for years on end, during which there was little official work he could do.

He kept himself busy in airshelters, dressed in Chinese garb, for his own wardrobe had burned. Van Gulik turned into an oriental scholar when he wasn't a diplomat and sorted samples of Chinese paper while he learned to mount scrolls. There was still another side to his mind; he was also Dutch.

Dutchmen were being tortured in the East Indies where the invader turned them from supermen into slaves, scurrying about in camps, in constant humiliation. Van Gulik *could* have been *there*, like many of his relatives and friends. He spent eight years in Java as a child, learned Malay, Javanese and Chinese there, perfected his Dutch at elementary school.

Who is Mr. Hendriks? Rather a stereotype, well known in the postwar Dutch environment. The man who is born in the lowlands, the former swamp that bordered the North Sea, since then secured behind dikes, who dutifully trains for officialdom in the colonies, zealously pursues a career in the tropics, loses all, is repatriated and lives out his life in gray despair. Van Gulik pushed his example to its limits. The pathetic bent human figure no longer has a family, he has even lost his mistress, and all hope for the future. It's a miracle that Hendriks can make himself get up in the morning, push himself through a dull working day, doesn't succumb to the destructive comfort of 'Schiedam gin' and the travesty of affection so amply provided in all Dutch cities by gaudy ladies displaying themselves in neonlit windows.

Van Gulik, even in his weakest aspect, was a hopeful man, for he gives his hero one potential way out, the great gift the East offers to all Westerners; realization of detachment. Not that Hendriks knows what's coming, but the possibility develops throughout the novel.

Most men win through parts of their lives, and lose in others. Van Gulik was mostly a winner. As a diplomat he rose to the rank of ambassador of an important country. As a scholar he won international acknowledgment, was a welcome guest at famous universities, became an authority on many subjects to the applause of his colleagues. As a novelist Van Gulik won wide acclaim. His own Chinese and Japanese versions of the Judge Dee mysteries sold well, proving the remarkable authenticity of his work. Reviews in the world's press were positive and admiring. He was recognized and respected wherever he went. Your Excellency in a chauffeured limousine, decorated and knighted by the queen, provided with tax-free income, dweller in palatial homes, father of four intelligent and zealous children, now what else could our protagonist possibly wish for?

There was also Mr. Hendriks. When Van Gulik lived in The Hague he would walk cold, wet streets, drink gin in cheap cafés where nobody knew him. Hendriks probably only showed up at odd moments, but it occurs to all of us, we become part of our environment, face the karma, the consequences of what our people did as a body, in the past that builds the present. Group karma, like personal consequences of private deeds, can cause much pain. There's no way in which to sidestep that pain. Hendriks lost his career and his family, and there's little left but a sweating body in a soaked raincoat and the shortlived glow of a few gins a day, drunk hastily in the company of non-caring others. What if Van Gulik had turned out to be another Mr. Hendriks, as could easily have happened, as *had* happened to some of his peers whom he had set out with, in the twenties and thirties. Would he have succumbed to national and private disaster? Become a semi-derelict, eking out useless days? Is there also purpose in the life of a loser? Lessons to be learned so that the spirit may soar?

Van Gulik accepted that challenge and wrote this one novel that seems so completely at odds with the rest of his work.

The Given Day can be read as just another thrilling mystery. Plenty happens at a fairly fast pace; there are several bad guys; some come to a spectacularly bad end and the rest are arrested. We meet with female sensuous grace and live through a prolonged, tricky chase in exotic settings. The good guy wins. But does he really? Mr. Hendriks crosses the finish as he set out at the start, in miserable quarters, bad health and with the same boring job. How can one win if fate is not improved? We Westerners must achieve; if we don't, we fail. So Hendriks fails.

But does he now? In Van Gulik's time the West had hardly heard about *koans* yet, the illogical questions asked by Zen masters, constructed to pierce the ever present duality the West has learned to live with. *Melt the snow on Mount Fuji*, Hendriks' Japanese torturer, the Military Police officer, ordered. How silly, does eternal snow ever disappear?

Nobody had heard yet about the peak experiences modern psychology is now investigating, and the ultimate goal of breaking egocentricity that leads to calmness, distance, the ultimate happiness that replaces the self.

Mr. Hendriks wouldn't have heard either, if his fate had not crushed his ignorance and resistance. He didn't solve the koan in the prison camp, and his demon, a former Zen disciple, hadn't either. The bad guy hands the question to his victim, before he himself is tried as a war criminal and hung. Hendriks continues the human quest. He has learned to give rather than take. He had to give much away in Java where he lost his comforts and his freedom. Does he start taking again after liberation? No, he shifts into neutral and waits to see what else fate may have in mind. And when other choices pop up and offer victory Hendriks steps back and wins peace of mind.

Here is another level of *The Given Day*. Van Gulik tests himself under circumstances that did not come about but that he could well envision. He no longer hides behind the mask of his other hero, the great Judge Dee, a historical representative of the T'ang Dynasty, who lived through the turbulence of his time to become a statesman at the court of the terrible Empress Wu and neutralized her perverted reign so that the Chinese people might live positive lives. Van Gulik also dropped the masks of the dignified ambassador, the celebrated scholar, the popular novelist.

The Given Day took the Dutch critics by surprise, and most judged harshly. They couldn't understand what the author had been up to and vindictively banished the book to the trash heap.

Van Gulik died of lung cancer, a disease that was already sapping his strength when he wrote *The Given Day*, so that Hendriks occasionally coughs and shivers. Van Gulik had put off his final attempt at self-analysis, but time was running short. In the text are signs that he bothered less about the exact attention to detail that marks his other work. He even changed the style of his illustrations, choosing abstract line figures rather than the flowing brush drawings inspired by the Chinese Ming style that had influenced Van Gulik's pictorial art for so long. He also made use of his knowledge of the Koran, and abstract Arab thought that enlivens Hendriks' enemies of the moment, lost souls, lead away from the truth by perversion.

I handed out some copies of the manuscript to American friends who were mostly disappointed. They wanted another Chinese thrilling tale, with a judge who shakes his sleeves, an obviously enlightened man who does away with evil, is helped by charming assistants who symbolize various sides of the practical and positive attitude that has made China last for more than four thousand years. The force of habit. More of the same. Once we see something we can appreciate we ask for endless repeats. Artistic development, however, is subject to change. Picasso painted for years, then tried to bake pots. Gillespie dropped traditional jazz patterns and switched to bop. We do it ourselves; we may continue in a given and successful direction for years on end until a crisis makes us veer off. What we do afterward may not be as easily understandable, or appreciated by others.

Van Gulik changed his song, but some of his previous motivation was retained. The Zen koan also showed up in the Dee novels, but Van Gulik never worked one out as completely as he does in *The Given Day*. Mr. Hendriks pours hot water in his teapot, and the ice on Mount Fuji melts. Hendriks melts his own shell, and realizes the answer to the human question. Why? For no reason. How? As best as he possibly can.

Judge Dee saw that too, in fairly well hidden nooks and crannies of Van Gulik's 'regular' mysteries. Judge Dee wore the tight mental corset made up by Confucian behavioral rules. Dee wanted no truck with Buddhist vagueness or the negation of Tao. Dee insisted on order and abhorred impractical philosophy, but the judge had his weak moments. In *The Lacquer Screen* Van Gulik quotes a Buddhist poem and makes Dee read and admire the context:

> *To be born means suffering and sorrow,*
> *To live means suffering and sorrow,*
> *To die, and never be reborn, is the only deliverance*
> *Of all suffering and sorrow.*

Sad? Even Dee didn't think so, for what dies here is the self, the constricting angle from which we view what seems to go on. Like Mr. Hendriks' self died when he poured the tea.

The present novel is out of print, with the exception of this very limited edition. It was never translated into many languages, as were Van Gulik's other books. The Dutch version appeared briefly, until devastating reviews swept it away, and the English version, printed privately in Malaya, was never distributed. The now available three hundred copies may complete some Van Gulik collections and perhaps, as a rare item, one day fetch a high price.

That doesn't matter much. More interesting is the glimpse the novel provides into the evolution of an exceptional man.

The Mugar Library, in Cambridge, Massachusetts, houses a collection of papers left by Van Gulik. One of the blue carton boxes contains numerous poems translated from Chinese and Japanese.

> *When I shall die*
> *Who will be sorry?*
> *Only the black mountain-crows perhaps*
> *They'll hop around my cold ashes.*
> *But the crows won't be truly sorry either.*
> *Their only regret is that they can't get at the funeral cookies*
> *Protected within the altar that shields my grave.*

Maybe the crows won't be disappointed after all, provided they make use of another hint that Van Gulik translated—if they slip through the crack hidden within the compulsion of having to choose between this or that.

> *You can't say that Tao exists*
> *and you can't say that Tao does not exist*
> *but you can find it in the silence*
> *when you no longer bother with important deeds.*

Janwillem Van de Wetering
Winter 1983, Maine, U.S.A.